PIPER ONE

A novel

GUY BLYTHMAN

Guy Blythman was educated at Millfield School, Somerset, and Southampton University and is currently based in the southwest London/northwest Surrey area. His interests include philosophy, theology, current affairs, classical music and, of course, writing. He goes on long country walks in order to be alone, but isn't averse to meeting people for a drink and a chat from time to time. He has at various times been a political activist, a civil servant, president of his school and college debating societies and secretary of diverse committees.

He is a member of Walton-on-Thames Wordsmiths, a local workshop group which aims to provide help and support to aspiring authors by offering constructive criticism and advice and suggesting possible markets. He has written for the *Doctor Who* fanzines *Mandria, Time-Space Visualiser* and *The Doctor's Recorder*.

Visit his website at www.guyblythman.com

Also by Guy Blythman in the same series of novels

Eye of the Sun God

ISBN 978-0-9557302-4-4

One

Jock Guthrie, thirty-nine years old and Chief Engineer on the Piper One oil rig, interrupted his routine daily check of the installation's systems to cross to the safety rail at the edge of the deck, fold his arms on top of it, gaze out over the North Sea and wonder for the hundredth time in the last few days whether his wife was having an affair.

During his last spell of leave, it had seemed to him she went through all the things they did together in a mechanical, automatic sort of way. There was a certain cheerfulness to her manner but he had the disturbing sensation it wasn't because of him. She wasn't unhappy so much as distant. That was as much of a danger sign.

Not for the first time, he considered giving up the job and going for something on the mainland. Things happened while husbands were away working on rigs. That had long been recognised, of course, as an occupational hazard; but it was always someone else they happened *to*, and when suddenly that was no longer the case you felt it like a kick in the teeth.

He found the less pleasant aspects of his profession, which had never bothered him before, suddenly coming to mind. Stuck out here in the middle of the cold, grey, windy sea doing hard, monotonous, often dangerous work. Was that what he was jeopardising his marriage for?

He felt a pang of guilt at the time he was taking to think over the matter. Best to keep it out of his mind if it wasn't to interfere with his work. He wanted out all right, but it wouldn't look good with any future employer if he got the sack.

He heard someone approach him and looked round. "You OK, Jock?" asked a colleague curiously.

He attempted to sound cheerful. "Aye, of course I am," he replied. He turned away abruptly and walked off, leaving the man staring after him.

He'd almost reached the rig's power plant, the next stop on his rounds, when the mobile phone in the pocket of his overalls rang. "Aye?" he answered.

"Jock? Drill room here. We're getting problems with Number Three. Looks like a bit of whiplash." There followed a slight pause. "Wait a moment, it's cleared. We're bringing her up to check there's no damage. Will you take a look at her?"

"Aye. Be with you in a minute."

He re-entered the superstructure of the rig and clambered down several flights of stairs to the drill room, a vast echoing chamber divided into two levels with a central well, formed by four metal columns, down which the drill descended before entering the hollow interior of one of the legs of the rig and passing down through it to the sea bed.

Previously, the drill had had to be hauled up and assembled manually, piece by piece. Now, it was a single huge mass of metal controlled more or less entirely by the computer on the upper level.

There were in fact a number of drills, each of which could be moved into position immediately if another had developed a fault.

Jock arrived in the drill room to see the slender, gleaming metal tube rising up through the opening in the floor of the chamber. He waited until the head of the drill, with its huge rotating cutters like those on a tin opener, was level with the inspection gantry built out from the wall.

He spoke into the mobile. "All right, stop her."

The drill stopped rising with a "clunk". Jock scrambled up the ladder to the gantry and across to it, his booted feet ringing out on the metal platform. He scanned the drill's titanium surface carefully. One of the cutters was slightly bent. Nothing much to worry about at the moment, but it could cause problems if it got worse. He reported his findings to the drill operator. "Reckon we'd better use another drill, and pull this one in for repairs. OK?"

"OK. Thanks, Jock."

Jock stepped away from the drill as it began to ascend into the ceiling. It disappeared into the hole above his head. He went back down the ladder.

At the bottom he paused, unable to exclude his marital problems from his thoughts. For a few minutes the matter of the drill had taken his mind off them, but now his worries were coming back.

If he could decide on a course of action it would put him at ease to some extent, prevent him feeling too screwed up. He'd have it out with Jeannie the next time he came home, he decided. If she was seeing someone during the two weeks he was out here on the rig, he'd offer to give up the job and see if it made any difference. Would it, though? He feared she might have got too high on whoever it was.

He was afraid that if he pushed the matter she might decide to jump. And he didn't want to lose her.

A letter might just precipitate her departure. He had to be there, to argue her into staying if at all possible. But if he waited even a day or two longer, she might in the meantime make up her mind to go. And experience told him that once a woman's mind was made up, it stayed made up.

What was he going to do?

Above him, the damaged drill was travelling to one side on a conveyor and its replacement was being swung into place. He looked up and saw it emerge through the opening in the ceiling and descend towards the one in the floor. He watched it idly as it came down.

Some time later, the drill operator was making an entry in his log book detailing the problem that had come up with the drill, and the steps taken to remedy it, when the internal phone rang.

It was the power plant. "Is Jock Guthrie with you? By my reckoning he should have got here a while ago. We've just rung his mobile, but he's not answering."

The drill operator frowned. "That doesnae sound like Jock. Hmmm...well, he was up here a few minutes ago. I asked him to give me a hand wi' the drill. Let me see if I can find him anywhere."

The drill could be left to its own devices for the time being. Briskly he descended the ladder, though it occurred to him there wasn't a great deal of point to his search; he didn't see why Guthrie would still be hanging around in the drill chamber.

But Jock was there. Or rather, his body was. It lay beside the rotating steel tube of the drill, its arms and legs sticking out at odd angles. And it *was* a body, because the drill had gone straight through his head, disintegrating it and splattering blood and fragments of brain, bone and flesh over an area the size of a tennis court.

Caroline Kent breezed into the Managing Director's office at International Petroleum's London headquarters and flashed him a cheery smile. "Morning, Marcus! Heard you got another job for me."

"You heard correctly," replied Marcus Hennig. "And it couldn't be more different from your last one."

The "last one" had been in Venezuela, on the edge of steaming tropical jungle. "Hmmm, let me guess...well, unless it's the South Pole, which it can't be because we're not allowed to drill there any more..."

She glanced at the model oil rig which took pride of place on his desk. "It's not one of those, is it?"

"Yes, m'dear. It's one of those."

Beside the model was a rolled-up sheet of laminated paper. Hennig spread it out on the desktop, and she saw it was a map. In the centre were a cluster of little black dots roughly halfway between the coast of north-east Scotland and that of Norway.

Hennig's thumb descended on a dot located some distance away from the others. "That," he said, "is Piper One. And some odd things have been happening there over the past few months."

"Like what?" asked Caroline, her interest immediately aroused, as it was by any new assignment. She took a seat, hooking one knee over the other.

"Tools and personal property gone missing, vital equipment apparently sabotaged, accidents which have caused serious injuries. On a number of occasions oil's been leaked into the sea, which has upset the green lobby. And just a couple of days ago, the chief engineer was killed."

"Oh," said Caroline. "Killed? How?"

"He was carrying out an inspection of the drill. Ten minutes or so after he was supposed to have finished he was found beside it with his head churned to pieces. Somehow or other it'd got under the thing."

Caroline grimaced, and a queasy shudder ran through her. "Ugh," she said simply.

"Indeed. He wasn't a pretty sight."

"Do they think it was deliberate?" she asked uneasily.

"In the light of everything else that's been going on, murder can't be ruled out."

"Is anyone under suspicion?"

"It could have been one of about half-a-dozen people. More, possibly. We've spoken to the police, of course. But there's no proof of foul play as yet. Same with all the other incidents. And the suspects have always strongly denied they did it. Of course if they *are* guilty, they would."

Caroline put on her thinking cap. "We *could* just be looking at a sequence of unfortunate events."

"I think it's a bit too much of a coincidence, don't you?"

"Perhaps. On the other hand, if morale among the workforce is low for some reason it could have an effect on the way people do their work; leading to mistakes of the kind you shouldn't make on an oil rig. And they're not admitting to it because, morale or no morale, they don't want to lose their jobs. They could move to another company's rig, but they don't want to, because we pay them such good wages."

"A death is a pretty serious matter. One or two people have already made clear they don't want to work on Piper One again."

"They've introduced partial automation on one of the rigs, haven't they? Was it this one?"

"As a matter of fact it was. Automation can *only* ever be partial, of course, because you'll always need a few people on hand in case anything goes wrong. But we've been able to reduce the number of personnel from two hundred to fifty, plus a doctor and his assistant.

"It's being speculated that that might have had something to do with it. The smaller and more isolated a community is the greater the tensions within it. Especially if it's a predominantly male one."

"Also, they may feel resentment at it," suggested Caroline. "It makes them feel less important. They could be afraid that one day the machines will take over altogether and they'll be out of work. I presume that when the automation was introduced, they were asked how they felt about it, what sort of impact they thought it would have on them?" It would have been good management; the sort of thing she'd have done.

"I think they were a little unhappy," Hennig admitted. "But they didn't have much choice. I mean, there's no sense in employing people where there's no need to. And as for them thinking it's made them redundant, that's bollocks. As I said, we'll always need a certain number of humans about the place."

"If it's sabotage," Caroline said, "then that's even more serious."

Hennig nodded. "Right now the police are open-minded on the subject. As to who's responsible...well, it could be a rival company, although it's probably taking things too far to suggest they'd resort to murder. They'd have to be using our own staff..."

"They couldn't be using anyone else. I don't see how they could have got on board the rig, let alone remained there for any length of time without someone noticing."

"That's right. Now, we've been asking the workforce to keep their eyes open, and report anything peculiar that might happen. Had to be done, of course. But I think it's only served to make people more suspicious of each other. However, apart from that I don't see what else, or what more, we can do. If it *is* sabotage."

"And I take it you want me to go out there, to see what I can find out, and talk the workers into staying?"

"I want this nipped in the bud, Caroline. Before it goes any further. We don't want to close the rig down and we don't want to go back to full manned operation, not if we can help it. In the long run automation could save this company thousands, maybe millions, of pounds, in personnel and other areas, by making the whole process more efficient. We want to know if we can go ahead with introducing it in all our plants, both new and existing. We need to find out if there could possibly be some reason other than sabotage for all that's been going on. If it is the automation, then we need to tell people to get their act together or go. There's no reason for them to feel aggrieved; they're still needed and they know that. And a plant that doesn't perform well, because they're not doing their job properly, is as bad as not having one at all.

"So I want you to get the feel of the place, find out if there's any problem with the way people are relating to each other. Stay as long as you need to, but no longer."

"When do I go?"

"In a couple of days' time. Now before I make the necessary arrangements, we need to get one or two things straight."

She looked at him curiously. "Like what?"

"As I said, it's a predominantly male environment. They do have women there, but only a few. It's a very physical sort of job, working on an oil rig, and with all due respect to your sensibilities women aren't up to many of the tasks involved. That's because they are, are as a rule, physically less strong than men." Caroline nodded her understanding, seeing no reason why she should take exception at this reference to what was, after all, simple biological fact. "I don't think it would be a good idea to have too many of them there in any case, because things would...things would happen."

"I can imagine," she said wryly.

"And, of course, with the overall reduction in the workforce their numbers have gone down even further. It wouldn't have mattered so much before."

"Now..." he coughed. “I want to assure you that the management take a pretty dim view of any, er, hanky-panky going on on a rig." The days when prostitutes had been flown in to keep the workers entertained while off duty – yes, it had been known – and the rig’s small cinema showed pornographic films were long gone. Though Caroline wondered if such things might actually have a useful role to play in reducing the very tensions of which they’d spoken, notwithstanding the distastefulness of the former in particular. It was probably because of the female personnel that the practice had been abandoned.

"But I still think there could be trouble. I mean, for one thing..." He hesitated.

Again she shot him an enquiring glance.

"I mean, you do tend to..."

"I tend to what?" she asked politely.

Another cough. "Turn heads."

"You mean more than turn heads." She laughed. "Well, they'd better learn to keep their hands off, or else."

"All the same, it'd be best if Chris Barrett goes with you on this one."

Chris was Caroline's companion and assistant on the majority of her troubleshooting missions. Despite her attempt at bravado she felt relieved. She knew that if anyone tried it on with her, Chris would give them a thump they'd never forget.

She nodded her agreement.

"To be honest, there's a danger your being on the rig may only make things worse," Hennig said.

"I don't have to take on the job, if you'd rather I didn't."

"You're the best troubleshooter we've got. But it's not a decision I'm happy making, so I'm leaving it up to you."

It was his words of praise that finally decided her. A warm glow of pride filled her breast. She had to live up to that.

"Well, I doubt if I'll come to any harm if Chris is there. Yes, I'll go."

"Of course," she added, "I could probably manage if anything untoward did happen."

"I'm sure you could," Hennig said. "Even so, I really don't like sending you out there." There seemed to be a genuine concern in his manner, something he'd never before displayed in his dealings with her, and Caroline was touched.

"I'll be all right," she smiled. "Honestly."

"It's just that in addition to forty or so lusty roughnecks, there seems to be a murderer about who puts people's heads under drills."

"*Seems*. We don't know for sure."

She looked at the map again, at the tiny black dot so far away from all the rest. Its very isolation made her shudder. "Why's it out there on its own like that?"

"It's a relatively new field, only discovered five years ago. Probably the last there'll be. We're hoping that in due course Piper One will be joined by about half a dozen other rigs.

"It's the most northerly, the most remote, of our oilrigs." He guessed at her thoughts. "But they're in constant touch with the mainland, and you'll have your mobile. There's a helicopter which comes from Inverness every four days bringing food and other supplies."

Somehow, these assurances did little to comfort her. But she couldn't turn back now. She knew what people would say if she did.

"Well," she said, trying to put a brave face on it, "I guess that's settled then."

*

There were no physical signs of injury or illness; but the seal was very, very dead. The huge, seemingly soulful eyes gazed up at Charlotte as she knelt over the body. She felt a surge of anger.

Hearing feet crunch on the shingle, she looked round and saw Kenny, like her wrapped up in dufflecoat, scarf and gloves against the biting northern wind. "Yep. The other one was the same. Its lungs were full of the stuff."

"This is the fifth time it's happened in one week," Charlotte sighed.

She rose and stood gazing out to sea to where she knew Piper One to be, her burning eyes staring intently into the distance.

She turned round suddenly, and Kenny saw them blaze fanatically in the way that always chilled him. "Bastards," she snarled. "The stupid bastards. They can't even do it *properly*."

The wind sent a slight ripple through her close-cropped brown hair. Kenny studied her face, thinking not for the first time that it would be attractive, in a coarse sort of way, if it wasn't marred by that perpetual scowl.

"We've got to do something about that rig," she said firmly.

"The company's said it's looking into it," Kenny reminded her.

Charlotte reacted immediately. "For God's sake, Kenny, that's what people always say. It usually means they're not going to do anything. You can't be so easily taken in by their spin."

"They don't want the pollution any more than we do. It looks bad for them. They'll have to do *something*."

"They shouldn't be producing that oil at all. Oil always pollutes." Charlotte hated the thick, clinging black liquid, its unnatural cloying smell.

"We've got to do something about it," she repeated. She turned and stomped up the beach towards a jumble of crudely constructed little huts.

Kenny knew her mind was made up. And that if her mind was made up, the others' would be too.

Two

The four of them sat round the table in the cramped, sparsely furnished little room. Its walls were of unpainted breezeblocks and it was more or less bare apart from the table and a few chairs. Warmth was provided by an old-fashioned portable electric heater; the blast of heat from its grille had a habit of trapping dust, tickling their noses and stinging their throats.

Not very luxurious surroundings, all in all. Charlotte reflected bitterly that she had known nothing better for some considerable time, and wasn't likely to in the foreseeable future. But she was prepared to put up with it.

She thought back over all that had led her to this. She'd been born into a reasonably conventional, and certainly not poor, upper middle class family. At the age of twelve she had been packed off to an expensive boarding school deep in the country. Not by inclination gregarious, she wasn't particularly popular there, but couldn't be said to be unpopular either. Her first three years at the school were fairly happy.

At the age of fifteen, she had discovered where her sexual allegiances lay when she formed a strong attachment, that went further than just friendship in its intimacy, to a girl in her House. She and Vicky spent as much time together as they could. Those were happy days for Charlotte, the best she had ever known. They came to an abrupt end when the two lovers were caught in bed together, hauled before the headmistress and summarily expelled.

It wasn't the expulsion itself which upset her so much as her family's reaction to the whole affair. Her father in particular was furious, beside himself with anger, shock and revulsion. In no uncertain terms she was forbidden to ever set eyes on her friend again. Every effort would be made to stop them having any sort of contact with each other. Since he suspected she would do her best to get round his injunction, he told her that if there was the slightest suspicion she was seeing Vicky he'd engage a private detective to make sure. Charlotte knew he was quite capable of that. Generally, his attitude towards her hardened. Her mother, explicitly or otherwise, tended to endorse it.

Charlotte had shed tears of anguish and frustration. Why couldn't they understand that it was a genuine and very deep love, a relationship from which both of them had benefited enormously, that had enriched their lives beyond measure? However much people might argue about whether homosexuality, male or female, was wrong Vicky had shown her more true kindness and affection than she'd ever had from her own family.

After initially hesitating, Charlotte had made the brave decision to walk out on her family as soon as she was sixteen, vowing never to have anything more to do with them. It was something they were quite happy to reciprocate.

She set herself up with Vicky in a bedsit in an area of London that was poor, but noted for its population of middle class left-wing intellectuals and political activists. The local authority was of the enlightened sort, going out of its way to recognise their relationship and ensuring the couple had every opportunity to enjoy full civil rights, so far a the law allowed, and a decent standard of living. Charlotte took a job as an assistant librarian with the local polytechnic.

Her new lease of life, which was what it felt like, was cruelly cut short when Vicky contracted a rare, terminal disease and died. For some time Charlotte was inconsolable to the point of hysteria. She knew she could never love another woman as much, and at the same time continued to be unattracted to men. She descended into bitter lethargy, performing badly at her job to the point where the polytechnic had no alternative but to sack her. After a long period on the dole she was taken on by a company which wasn't too fussy about the kind of people it employed, yet paid them little more than starvation wages.

Charlotte needed a cause, something to lift her up out of the rut into which she had sunk. Eventually she found one. She had come to hate a society which didn't allow you to have the kind of relationship you wanted – forgetting that ultimately it had been the hand of Fate rather than of Man which had deprived her of her happiness – and seemed riddled with cruelty and hypocrisy. It also did terrible things to the natural environment.

All her anger and hatred at the injustice of the world seemed crystallised in this one issue. An order which insisted on ruining the very earth itself, the very air people breathed, the sea they swam in – the things they needed for life and health – must be utterly vile and wicked, deserving of total destruction. This, she knew, must be her aim. She wanted to destroy the system rather than reform it. Some within the movement, along with plenty outside it, found her very real hatred of the establishment and its supporters disturbing and distasteful. What they didn't understand was that that hatred was all she had left.

She came out of her reverie just as Dave started to speak. "What exactly have you got in mind, Charlotte?"

"I say we hit that rig. I say we blow Piper One right out of the fucking water. We have the equipment, or we can get hold of it fairly easily." She glanced at the muscular figure beside her. "That's where Sean's contacts will come in very useful."

Like many ex-soldiers, Sean Bailey had had trouble adjusting to civilian life. Now at last he, like Charlotte, had found a cause. And what in particular pleased him about it was the opportunity it provided to use all his old army skills.

His eyes were glinting. Yes, it was clear he was relishing the chance to point guns at people again.

Kenny looked less enthusiastic. "We've never done anything like it before."

"There's got to be a first time. Or there'll never be a second, a third, a fourth, and so on. We decided a long time ago that just marching from A to B wasn't achieving very much and we needed to do so something more. Let’s walk the walk, yeah?" She didn’t mean yet another march.

"What about the crew?"

"We won't kill them if that can be avoided. Don't worry, I've got it all worked out." Charlotte had in fact planned the operation, and discussed it with Sean, in meticulous detail some time previously. She proceeded to go over it again for the benefit of the others, with an air that suggested she regarded the matter as already decided.

Dave was sceptical. "I don't see how we're going to get anywhere near the fucking place. They patrol the area around an oil rig pretty thoroughly."

"Don't worry. No-one's going to question our credentials. And if they do, they'll find them impeccable. As far as they're concerned we'll be a scientific survey ship checking pollution levels in the sea. Anyone they ask will confirm our identity and testify as to our good faith." It didn't require a great deal of effort to pose as a legitimate scientific foundation. Because that was what they were – officially.

"All the same," Charlotte went on, "I'm taking the precaution of hiding the guns and stuff, just in case anyone decides to come on board and snoop around." The equipment would be concealed in a secret compartment within one of the ship's bulkheads. In order to find them the authorities would have to painstakingly dismantle most of the vessel's fittings, and she couldn't see them going to such trouble if there had been nothing much to excite their suspicions in the first place.

"Any questions?" she asked afterwards.

"We'd only make the pollution worse, you realise that? If we blow up the rig then the oil leaks into the sea."

"I'm well aware of the risks, Kenny. I wouldn't be suggesting we do this unless the gains outweighed the costs. What counts is the message we're sending out. Sure, we run the risk of polluting a large chunk of sea if we go ahead with my plan. But if people like us don't put our balls on the table it'll be the whole world that's screwed, the way things are going. The long-term psychological effect of our action will outweigh the immediate physical damage. The public will have the importance of the issue made clear to them, because they'll be wondering what could have led us to take such an…extreme step. And the companies will be forced to spend a lot more money on security, which they won't be happy about especially in time of recession. The government too. We weaken our enemies by making them overstretch their resources."

"I still don't think..." Kenny broke off, contemplating the table unhappily. She eyed him with disdain.

"Well, let's put it to the vote," she said crisply. Everyone raised their hands except Kenny. After a moment he too followed suit, trying not to look too obviously uneasy. He always felt uncomfortable about making clear his doubts regarding a course of action Charlotte had suggested.

"Great," she beamed. "That means the only thing we now need to decide is when."

She'd already prepared a press release, to be delivered anonymously of course. "The following is a statement from the General Committee of the Children of Gaia. In the early hours of this morning our organisation carried out a successful attack on the oil production platform Piper One. This target was selected as a protest against the continuing pollution of our planet by the oil corporations and their allies in government.

"We will continue to attack oil installations, and all other symbols of capitalist industrial society, wherever possible, until the politicians and the tycoons cease their wanton destruction of the global environment. We appeal to the public to understand and support us in our aims and not be swayed by the spurious arguments of those who insist that capitalism, despite its faults, is the only option. That is the end of this message."

"Never been on an assignment like this before," said Caroline. She'd been on a rig once, not long after she'd first joined the company, on a visit intended to familiarise employees who'd been marked out as future managers with its various operations, but they'd stayed no more than a few hours.

"I'm afraid you're going to have to leave your wardrobe behind," said Chris, a stockily-built young man of about her own age with wavy dark hair and a pleasant, rounded, vaguely handsome face. "An oil rig isn't the most glamorous place on Earth."

That was the least of Caroline's worries, although she didn't give voice to the others. Gazing out through the window of her office at the London skyline, she found herself counting the number of tower blocks she could see.

The remoteness of Piper One continued to worry her. She thought of what seemed to be happening there, the engineer's gruesome death under the drill, and again felt a cold shiver of dread.

"Hennig's worried I'm going to be molested by the testosterone brigade," she said.

"You'll have me to look after you," Chris reminded her.

"I'm sure I'm grateful for that."

In fact, her apprehension was already beginning to dispel as the thought of taking up the challenge and meeting it became uppermost in her mind. Her spirits were rising as she headed down to the canteen for lunch.

There two senior executives, Decker and Reece, the latter a recent recruit to the company from another sector of industry, were chatting to each other as they took their trays from the stack and joined the queue. "I hear our International Operations Manager is off on her travels again," said Decker, using the official title of Caroline's post.

"That trouble at the oil rig?"

"Uh-huh. Rather her than me. Those places give me the creeps. In the middle of nowhere, with all that bloody sea around them; all sorts of things could go on there without anyone knowing."

He sighed. "Do you honestly think it's sensible to send a woman out there, to a rig full of men? Especially one like her."

"How d'you mean?"

"Well, look at her." He nodded towards the attractive blonde as she carried her tray to one of the tables, to join the group of colleagues already seated there.

Reece eyed Caroline appreciatively. "I see what you're getting at."

"It's asking for trouble," Decker grumbled. "But no, she has to prove she's not afraid of the risks, she can handle the job as well as any man."

"Mind you," he added, "she did all right in that South American business."

Reece was intrigued. "What South American business?"

"You'll think I'm having you on…oh, what the hell. She got kidnapped by terrorists who were trying to undermine the company. Ended up in the den of this drug baron who was funding them; the guy seems to have taken a fancy to her. She escaped – no trouble at all for the Amazing Caroline – called the authorities, and they managed to get a trace on his hideout. He got away, but his whole operation was busted and nobody's heard anything of him since. The number one druglord in that part of the world, bigger than Escobar.

"That's not all there is to it, either. Somehow, she then managed to get herself kidnapped by a tribe of Indians and spirited off into the rain forest. Didn't manage to get back to civilisation for months. At least that's what she says. I have a feeling it's not quite the whole truth."

"You're joking," said Reece. He shook his head firmly. "No, I don't believe it."

"There are plenty of other stories I could tell you about her. Sometimes I'm not sure *I* believe them."

"Well if she's some sort of female James Bond she shouldn't have any trouble sorting out this oil rig thing."

"I hope not," muttered Decker darkly. "It may be a lot closer to home but that doesn't mean it's any safer." He pursed his lips. "I just have this general sense of foreboding about the whole business."

Three

Chris stood with his travel bag slung over his shoulder in the departure lounge at Heathrow, waiting for Caroline to join him. Well, here we are again, he thought.

How many times had the two of them done this sort of thing now? About a dozen, he reckoned. Some of those assignments had led them into danger, others had not. But usually, their efforts had resulted in some kind of wrong being put right. And it hadn't just been the company that had benefited.

He felt a surge of pride at the things they'd done together. One of them really ought to write a book about it some day. The thing was, would anybody believe it? Maybe if it were done as fiction...

Caroline bounded up to him sporting a tam o'shanter. "Hoots mon, we're off tae bonnie Scotland."

"Very nice," he said.

"I just thought I'd get into the spirit of things. Now have you got everything you need?"

"Of course," he replied, smiling tolerantly.

"Should hope so. If you want something while you're there you can't exactly pop out to the shops."

"I gathered that."

"Jolly good. So, are you looking forward to it?"

"It'll be different."

"Sure will."

They stood talking and watching their fellow travellers go by until the time came for them to board their flight. A few minutes later they were in the air.

Another airport, another plane. Another destination.

The journey was uneventful, and would have been boring for Caroline if not for the paperback novel she had had the foresight to bring along with her. Chris wasn't much company, spending most of the time chatting up the girl in the seat in front of him.

Three hours later they had touched down at Aberdeen and were approaching the checkout counter. Caroline had the tam o'shanter, which she had worn throughout the flight, perched on her head at a jaunty angle. "I shouldn't wear that here if I were you," said Chris. "They won't like it."

"Why not?"

"They may think you're patronising them. I had an uncle who married a Scotswoman. He went to a do her family were organising dressed in a kilt. They took him aside and said he was a nice guy and they were very fond of him and all that but they didn't like him wearing the kilt."

Sulkily Caroline took the hat off. She'd always thought the Scots were supposed to have a sense of humour.

In the foyer they were met by two executives, a young man and woman in smart business suits who introduced themselves as Martin Glenister and Helen McVinnie. The four of them then drove in

Glenister's car to the company's onshore base, a jumble of concrete boxes with a small airfield nearby where an orange and black helicopter sat waiting, its rotors at rest for now. They alighted from the car outside the main administration building, and went through the swing doors into Reception.

There a man in his late forties, big and powerfully built with a craggy face and dark hair greying at the temples, in a workman's donkey jacket was pacing slowly up and down with his hands in his pockets. He looked round as Glenister called out to him. "Jim?"

They went over to the man and Glenister introduced him to the two new arrivals. "This is Jim MacDuggan, superintendent at Piper One. Jim, meet Caroline Kent and Chris Barrett." He explained who they were and why they were there.

MacDuggan shook Caroline's hand somewhat indifferently. "Ah, yes, I've heard of you," he said. The tone to his voice showed he wasn't exactly overjoyed to see her here. She was somewhat thrown by it, the more so because she wouldn't have expected him to be so overtly hostile in the presence of management. It made her feel very unsettled. It registered with her that when Glenister had performed the introductions there had been something apprehensive about his manner.

She recovered her composure. "Oh, er, have you?" she responded, smiling politely.

"Your fame has spread far and wide," McDuggan said. "We've all heard about your amazing exploits."

Caroline did her very best to appear modest.

"I've also heard," the superintendent went on, "that you like things done the way you want." Again that tone of icy hostility. In it was an element almost of threat.

"That's a tautology, you know," smiled Caroline. MacDuggan made a non-committal noise.

As for Chris, the foreman completely ignored him.

Martin Glenister gave an embarrassed cough. "Um, how about something to eat? We've laid on a meal for you both in the conference room."

"That's very nice of you," said Caroline. "Yes, why not?"

"Do you want to join us, Jim? It'll save you waiting till you get back to the rig."

MacDuggan grunted an affirmative.

The superintendent barely spoke to them during the meal, apart from when he expressed, in highly patronising tones, his conviction that they would sort out matters at Piper One to everybody's satisfaction. Every few minutes he could be caught looking at them with an expression of barely disguised enmity. McVinnie and Glenister were clearly annoyed by his behaviour, and tried to drop hints to that effect.

Chris wondered how MacDuggan could be so coldly hostile to a girl with Caroline's looks, who he had never met before. It didn't make sense.

Afterwards McVinnie and Glenister, who both had urgent business to attend to, excused themselves, leaving Chris and Caroline waiting in Reception for the taxi that would take them to their hotel. MacDuggan was there too, staring out through the glass sliding doors for a glimpse of the bus to the heliport.

Once Martin and Helen had gone, Chris and Caroline looked at each other with raised eyebrows. "I don't think Mr MacDuggan is all that happy about our involvement," muttered Chris.

"Yes, that was certainly the impression I got."

"I think I'll have it out with him," Caroline decided.

"Be careful," muttered Chris.

She strode briskly over to MacDuggan. "May I have a word with you?" she asked. "In confidence."

He gazed down at her in the manner of someone confronted by something lowly but vaguely intriguing. Then he moved over to a quiet corner of the foyer, indicating by a curt jerk of his head that Caroline should follow. She complied.

She folded her arms. "You don't like me, do you Mr MacDuggan?"

At first the foreman was impassive. Then his lips twitched to form an insolent smile.

"I was just wondering if you could possibly tell me why. I know I have to grit my teeth and make an effort to get on with people I don’t somehow seem to form a chemical combination with, but it does help if there is one.”

By now MacDuggan had realised he was dealing with a personality as strong as his own. He locked horns.

"That oil," he said in a soft, quiet, but passionate voice, "belongs to us, not you bloody Sassenachs."

For a brief moment, Caroline was taken aback by the remark and by the strength of the emotions behind it. Then she rallied.

"That oil," she said sternly, "is a finite resource which the whole world needs, and needs badly. Still. It's hardly fair that one small country, which is what Scotland would be if it was independent, should have control of it. Presumably you'd do what you liked with it, because there wouldn't be any point in being a separate nation if you couldn't use your resources how you wanted. If people thought there was the slightest chance of you hogging too big a share of the stuff, it'd be a good incentive for them not to let you start out on your own."

The highly pertinent point she was making was evidently lost on MacDuggan. "Don't think you can come here and tell us how to run everything. There's been enough of that. Things are different now."

"Look, Mr MacDuggan. I'm quite happy to admit Scotland has been badly treated in the past – "

She wasn't to be allowed to finish. "Well, now you know what it feels like," MacDuggan said with relish.

He was probably referring to the peculiar, and unjust state of affairs in which the English can no longer legislate for Scotland and Wales – an arrangement Caroline, like most English people, had no particular quarrel with – but have to submit to the jurisdiction of those Scottish and Welsh MPs who still sit at Westminster. The discrimination was offensive to Caroline's mind, and made more so by the fact that in the beginning at any rate some Scots had openly gloated over the situation, the feeling of national self-assertion having brought out their worst instincts.

"Yes, I do," she replied. "That's how I know it's wrong."

She leaned towards him to emphasise what she was about to say. "I should remind you that this is an international company."

"Owned by English," said MacDuggan. He pronounced the word as if speaking of something utterly repulsive and contemptible.

"Some of the shareholders are Scots, like my number two at Personnel, or Welsh. And we've always known that if we want things to run smoothly, we've got to pay attention to people's sensibilities. Respect different nationalities and backgrounds. That goes for the way people treat...*English* as much as it does anything else.

"And since technically I'm your superior, you shouldn't really be talking to me in this way, should you?"

MacDuggan glared at her defiantly.

"Needless to say, I'm extremely concerned at your attitude and I'll be reporting this conversation to senior management."

"You do that," said the foreman coolly.

"And on a personal level, I object to being called a "bloody Sassenach.""

She started to walk off, then paused and turned back to him. When she spoke her tone of voice was more friendly. "You're angry because you don't think devolution goes far enough. But independence wouldn't work either, believe me. I did a little historical research before I came here – I felt it was a wise thing to do somehow – and it seems the Union happened in the first place because there was no alternative. Because economically, if only economically, Scotland was so much weaker than England.

"I feel sorry for you in a way. You've always had to be second fiddle to us, because that's the way things are. And you don't like that, because you're a proud people. You've good reason to be." They'd produced so many engineers, scientists, writers, and educationalists, and been instrumental in building up the British Empire, even if you didn't think that was anything to be proud about. "You're creative, cultured, hard-working..."

"Ah, how sweet of you to say so."

"You're welcome. But I was going to say that there are some things you just have to accept. There's nothing to be gained from moaning about them."

"I'm sure we need *your* sympathy."

Chris had come up beside her. "We've got to work together on this," he told MacDuggan. "We can't afford to fall out. I'm sure you want to solve the problems Piper One seems to have as much as we do."

MacDuggan stalked off, the two of them gazing helplessly after him. The sliding doors swished shut.

Shaking her head sadly, Caroline turned away.

Outside the building MacDuggan paused on his way to the bus stop, frowning. For a moment his face twisted fiercely, like that of someone in pain.

Be careful, he told himself. *They* need you. You won't be helping things if you get yourself sacked.

He moved on.

Four

Caroline was telling Chris what MacDuggan had said to her. ""Now you know how it feels like,"" she quoted.

"Arsehole."

"And he called us bloody Sassenachs." Her blue eyes flashed at the insult.

She tried to understand MacDuggan's feelings; to find if possible some explanation for his passionate, bigoted hatred. What was it motivated that kind of nationalist?

The problem seemed to be twofold. Firstly, that Scotland had for so long been denied independence. There were, as Caroline had pointed out, sound historical and practical reasons for that, things which the English could not reasonably be blamed for. That the partnership was an unequal one, with those south of the border acting as if "English" and "British" were the same thing, was inevitable and understandable seeing that England was the driving force behind the UK, constituting most of its population and industry and thus the bigger economy. It was irksome for patriotic Scots to be trapped in a situation so offensive and frustrating to them. But there wasn't much that could be done about it.

Secondly, the English had sometimes made jokes about the Scots. Those jokes were not necessarily nasty, and sometimes disguised, if anything, a certain affection. The problem seemed to be the combination of the two grievances. There appeared to be an unwarranted assumption that the two things, each perhaps acceptable on its own, amounted when taken together to something that wasn't.

The trouble was, it might come about in human affairs that what had been done originally for bad reasons – racial prejudice and a wish to dominate – might, at a later stage, have to be done for good ones. However, some people seemed unable to make the distinction. For nationalists of MacDuggan's bent, Scotland's being part of the United Kingdom in the twenty-first century was a logical part of a trend which went back to Edward I's wars of conquests in the thirteenth and fourteenth.

These days people like MacDuggan were something of an anachronism. It probably hadn't been more than a relatively small minority of Scots who had been really nasty over devolution, bullying English-born children at school and ostracising those compatriots who had married English spouses. In any case, with fears about corruption and growing social and economic problems their triumphalism had since been muted by a realisation that it wasn't what it was cracked up to be. Many Scots were actually leaving Scotland, so that immigration – including from England – needed to be encouraged in order to keep the economy going, which meant you couldn't afford to be too chauvinistic or xenophobic. Worry about the country's difficulties caused people to overeat, or seek comfort in foods which tasted nice but weren't very nutritious, with the result that the Scots were among the unhealthiest people in Europe. Caroline felt genuinely sorry for them, in a way she could honestly say wasn't patronising. Somehow they deserved better.

But as for the oil being Scotland's..."I'd say that was a bit of a dead issue these days," Chris opined. It had been one since the collapse of prices in the mid-1980s brought an end to the initial North Sea oil boom. The black stuff was no longer an asset worth waging nationalist campaigns over.

A group of oilmen came along, no doubt on their way to catch the next flight to the rig. They stopped to chat. "I see you've met the Chief," grinned one. They must have been passing by when Caroline had her run-in with MacDuggan and overheard something of the conversation.

"I'll say I have," she muttered.

"He's no' so bad really," said another, but she had the impression this was said principally out of loyalty.

"He's a funny character, that I'll admit. Loves the job, though. He's more or less permanently on Piper, while everybody else goes home every two weeks. In fact he once spent a whole year out on one of the rigs, alone."

Caroline's eyebrows shot up. "A *year*?"

"Well, the best part of one. From March to December. We managed to persuade him to come home for Christmas."

"You're joking," gasped Chris.

"No, I'm no'. You're no' really allowed to do it, but he wanted to and he got his way. Says a lot about what the management think of him.

"I don't think anyone else could have done it. We all like the job, most of the time anyway. But him..."

"Maybe he's mad," said Chris. "Or perhaps it was spending so long out there...no, I guess to do that he'd have to have been a bit barmy in the first place."

"He volunteered for the job just after his wife died. He hasn't been the same since she passed on."

"Evidently not," Caroline sighed. But despite herself she felt a strong pang of sympathy.

"His job's the only thing that keeps him going. That and his country."

Nodding politely to them, the oilmen moved on. Once they were out of earshot Chris lowered his voice. "Maybe MacDuggan's the one who's trying to wreck the rig. If Scotland can't have the oil – Scotland alone – then nobody can."

"It's possible," frowned Caroline. The suggestion seemed a bit far-fetched to her. She wasn't sure Chris himself had meant it seriously. Unless, of course, MacDuggan *was* mad.

"Well," she said brightly, "let's see what the police have to say about it, shall we?"

*

Superintendent Mark Lewars of Aberdeen CID, within whose remit fell crimes committed on offshore oil installations, received Caroline courteously enough. But she sensed a certain barrier between the two of them, as if Lewars felt her presence was mostly superfluous and that her visit to him could achieve little concrete result.

He was quite possibly right. It was little more than routine, on an assignment like this one, although a face-to-face meeting, as well as being polite, also had greater psychological effect.

He directed her to a chair. The window was slightly open, letting in a pleasant sea breeze, on which drifted the crying of seagulls.

"So," she opened, "what actually happened?"

"Guthrie? He was called to the drill chamber on his mobile and asked to take a look at the drill because there was something wrong with it. After he'd fixed it, the drill operator assumed he'd left the chamber. The operator remained in the control room for ten minutes or so, then when the power plant, where Guthrie was supposed to have gone next, called and asked where he was he went down to look for him and found the body.

"The operator *could* have gone down and killed him during that time, if he'd still been in the drill chamber for some reason. But why? There doesn't seem to be a clear motive. Everything suggests the fellow's thoroughly reliable and trustworthy."

"So at the moment you're not treating the death as suspicious?"

"No. Not unless any further evidence emerges, and we've already conducted a thorough investigation into the matter. It's the same with all the other incidents. Some of them obviously were deliberate, but that doesn't mean the...death was, too. And where something was stolen or wilfully damaged we've never been able to identify the culprit."

"I'm inclined to think Guthrie must have slipped or something," he said after a brief pause. "And probably knocked himself out."

"What could he have slipped on? Was there any oil spilt on the floor? I doubt it, not in the drill chamber; it'd have no reason to be there. And he would have taken care *not* to slip. You have to be careful in a job like that."

And even if he had slipped, the probability of him landing with his head directly underneath the drill seemed somehow too great. It was possible, of course. But...

Caroline asked if Guthrie had had a history of illness. Could he have blacked out suddenly or suffered a heart attack? There was nothing in his medical records which suggested he could. And if that was the explanation, why had it happened at the very moment when it would have been most dangerous for him; when he'd been standing next to the point at which the drill, descending swiftly, would pass through the floor of the chamber? What reason had he to have been standing there at all?

She shared her thoughts with Lewars.

"So you believe it was murder, Miss Kent?"

"I think you do."

The policeman shrugged. "You're free to draw your own conclusions where that's concerned, Miss."

"If someone had knocked him out, and then moved him so his head was under the drill, the drill would have...well, it would have left no trace of any injury, would it? I mean…" Once more she shuddered.

"I guess you're right," murmured the Superintendent. "Look, Miss, I really don't think there's much you can do. Obviously we'll let you know if any new evidence does turns up."

"It's not entirely a police matter," she said. "It's my job to sort out problems like this for the company. And you never know, I just might be able to find out something useful."

For Lewars to tell her anything more than what he had would be breaking confidentiality. There was no reason however why she shouldn't make enquiries among the rig personnel, if it helped her investigation in any way. That would be legitimate, internal company business.

"Well," she said, rising and shaking Lewars' hand, "thankyou for your time. Now I must be off, I've a helicopter to catch."

For her sojourn on the rig, she had settled for clothes which would be sensible in the circumstances; jeans, sweater and a pair of Doc Martens. Chris was equipped in much the same way. Each crammed a few essential possessions into a holdall.

The weather was cold, clear and sunny as they walked out to where the company helicopter sat waiting for them on the tarmac. The pilot greeted them with a cheerful "Welcome aboard!"

The flight was OK, though occasionally the wind got up and buffeted the helicopter uncomfortably. The view from the window was beautiful in a stark sort of way, but boring. Mostly sea, miles and miles of choppy grey sea stretching away to infinity on all sides. But here and there the outline of a rig broke the monotony, and in places they dotted the skyline. Caroline counted thirty in all.

"That's the rig where Mr MacDuggan stayed for a year," the pilot shouted, jerking his head to the left. Glancing through the window they saw it, about a quarter of a mile to the west. Barbed wire now festooned the ageing, rusty structure, which was evidently no longer in use.

Ten minutes passed. "There she is," the pilot yelled.

On the horizon a small black speck had appeared. As they drew closer it resolved itself into the shape of a rig. Three huge, cylindrical concrete legs supported the multi-layered superstructure two hundred feet above the surface of the sea. There were cranes for unloading supplies when the consignment was too big to be carried on board a helicopter but the sea calm enough for a ship to make the journey. A long boom jutted out from the side of the rig at a thirty degree angle, carrying the burner in which the excess gas produced during the drilling process was disposed of. A jet of flame forty feet long blazed from the mouth of the steel tube. Emblazoned on the side of the rig was the name Piper One accompanied by the silhouette of a Highlander with bagpipes.

They could see black, ant-like figures moving about on the deck, or clustered on the helipad to greet them.

They had already put on their donkey jackets, and now the co-pilot tossed them a pair of safety helmets. The helicopter banked, swung out over the rig, then began to descend, the pitch of its engines changing. It settled down to land with a slight bump.

The steps were lowered, and Chris and Caroline said their thanks to the pilot and alighted. Caroline gulped in the cool, refreshing sea air and felt it invigorate her, making her forget her worries. She savoured the touch of the wind on her face.

A little group of people, MacDuggan among them, stood nearby. "Hello again," Caroline said to the foreman, making an effort to be pleasant. She had to raise her voice a little above the wind.

MacDuggan nodded briefly. He indicated the man next to him, a red-haired giant with a rugged, cheerful face. "This is Jamie Grant, my number two. He'll show you where everything is."

Behind them the helicopter's rotors started up. It took off, banked, and veered away from the rig. Soon it was a rapidly dwindling little dot in the vastness of the sky.

The rig had its own helicopter, sitting on the deck a hundred yards from where they stood; no doubt this was necessary in case someone fell ill or was injured in an accident and had to be ferried to the mainland. Caroline was glad of its presence; it made her feel less cut off from civilisation.

Jamie Grant introduced them to a few of the other oilmen, while MacDuggan stood in the background letting him get on with it. She could sense their interest in her, and the vibrations she was picking up were a little disturbing. It was unfortunate that the tight jeans she was wearing showed off her behind and legs to best advantage.

"Now let's get inside, in the warm," said Grant. They headed for one of the doors leading into the superstructure.

It seemed most of the rig's workforce were out to greet them, all craning their necks to get a glimpse of the famous Caroline Kent. They were just out of earshot. But if Caroline could have heard the comments they were making, she would not have been surprised.

"Tasty. *Verrry* tasty."

"Jesus Christ! What did she do to fix that drug baron character, make his balls burst?"

"She's a Sassenach."

"So what? You can still screw her."

"Reckon ye've got a chance then?"

"All right, lads, back to work," shouted MacDuggan. Immediately the men turned and trooped back inside, all thought of their glamorous visitor immediately forgotten.

"I was going to take them to the canteen, Chief," said Grant. "Give them a bite to eat before showing them round the place."

MacDuggan grunted his assent, then halted, turned on his heels sharply and went off. Grant made no comment, used to his superior's peculiar ways.

The canteen was nearly empty, everyone else being at work, and as they sat down to eat Caroline thought it safe to bring up the reason why she was here.

"Ah, yes, I was meaning to tell you. Ask me about all that. You won't get much out of the Chief."

"We gathered that," Chris said.

Caroline let her colleague open. "It could be that automation isn't a good idea in that it results in too small a working community, and things are getting more tense as a result. That's something we're here to confirm, or otherwise."

Grant shook his head firmly. "No, it's not that at all. Some people had to be laid off and they weren't happy about it. But I mean, all of us know you can't turn everything over to a bloody machine. As long as our jobs are safe we don't mind. The real problem right now is these funny goings-on. If they carry on, and no-one can find out who's doing it, we're all going to pack up and go home." He looked hard at Caroline. "You're our last chance."

"I won't let you down," she smiled.

"So what do you think explains these, er, goings-on?" Chris asked.

"I don't know," Grant sighed. "Some of them may be genuine accidents. And things do get lost, of course, no matter how careful everyone is to look after their tools. No-one's been caught in the act, you see, which makes it hard to find out the truth. What I'm certain of, though, is that people *have* made mistakes."

Caroline sensed she could confide in him. "You mean, not just because you do from time to time? That suggests to me the sabotage, if that's what it is, is having a bad effect on morale. It's what the person responsible would want."

"About the man who was killed," said Chris. "Jock Guthrie. Is there any reason why he might have committed suicide? I don't like to suggest it, but we have to consider every..." He glanced at Caroline for approval, and she nodded back.

Grant pursed his lips. "Well, I'll tell you something; he wasn't quite himself in the couple of days before he was killed. He was very quiet and he seemed to forget things, which was way out of character for him believe me. It was obvious he had something on his mind. Could be something happened, domestically, while he was on leave. It's not uncommon for wives to start seeing someone else because their husbands are away so much of the time. Whatever it was, it was obviously screwing him up.

"So it's *possible*. I'll say no more than that."

"Would you tell your boss I'd like to speak to the whole workforce, at some convenient point." Giving everyone a pep talk was part of Caroline's usual strategy when on an assignment like this.

Grant showed them round the rig, pointing out the places where the accidents had occurred. They came to the drill chamber. Caroline felt a pang of unease at the thought she was standing in the very place where the gruesome death had occurred. She studied its layout closely, trying to picture the scene at the moment Guthrie was killed.

As the venue for her talk she chose the cinema, which could double as a lecture hall. The workforce had not needed to be prompted to attend, she noted.

MacDuggan said a few brief words of introduction, then she stood up to speak.

"Wha-hae," someone roared. "Get 'em off."

MacDuggan gave the man a quelling look, and he fell instantly silent.

Caroline did her stuff. "My name's Caroline Kent and I'm International Operations Manager (2). You all know why I'm here. It's important you don't let what's been happening affect your morale. If you do then the saboteur, if there is one on board, wins. Now my job is to sort things out if I can. In the meantime, I'm asking you all to be patient. Until we know what the problem is, please do your best not to let it interfere with your work. You don't like the way things are, so it's all the more important we resolve the issue. But for that to happen, you'll need to be honest with me. I should be here for the best part of a week, maybe longer. So if you have any worries or want to talk about something in confidence, come and see me or my number two Chris Barrett." She glanced at Chris, who stood up and smiled at their audience.

"That's all I have to say for now. So if you've quite finished looking at my legs, we can all get on with our work."

The men filed out.

"Do you think that went well?" she whispered to Chris.

"You said all you needed to. The trouble is, they're more interested in your – undoubted assets than in what you can do to solve the mystery." He wondered if being honest about it was the correct approach, or not.

"Well if they don't take this business seriously they may as well all hand in their notices."

"I take it we're not going to leave it at that, though."

"Of course not. We're going to talk to a few people, and see what we can learn; find out if there's anybody here who's covering up something."

Standing just outside the door, MacDuggan listened suspiciously to their lowered voices.

"There's one big obstacle we have to get round," Caroline sighed. "You mentioned it just now."

"You mean, your being a babe?"

"If you put it like that, yes. I don't feel safe here, Chris."

He summed up the problem eloquently. "It's obvious they're all dying to get inside your knickers. Any man would if he got the chance." She gave him an odd look, pretending she didn't know what he was talking about. "Besides, they don't get an awful lot of female company. Of course, that doesn't necessarily mean they'll try it on. But it could make our job here more difficult."

"I think I'll go and talk to a few of the women. I guess I won't have any problems there. Meanwhile, I want you to try the men. See if you can learn anything in the bar. Drink can loosen people's tongues, even if it's only lemonade." For safety reasons oil companies generally tended to ban alcohol from rigs.

"Come and find me later, and we'll compare notes. I'll probably be in my room." She made to go.

Chris stopped her. "Caz?"

"Yes?"

"I won't let any of them muck about with you. You know that, don't you?"

She smiled warmly at him. "I think I do."

On arriving at the bar, Chris found that most of the rig's workforce seemed to have gravitated there. They needed the solace drink offered. On top of the recent disturbing events, the arrival of the glamorous and nubile young woman had only served to increase the tension. It ought to have cheered them up, but instead many of them felt nervous and unsettled.

Three or four roustabouts sitting at a table at the side of the room eyed Chris as he came in, crossed to the bar and ordered his lemonade.

"I reckon they're having it off," said one. "Got to be."

The man next to him grunted offhandedly, absorbed in a daydream in which he was trying out a variety of sexual practices and positions on Caroline, who was naked except for an oil worker's safety helmet.

"Hey, pal," Chris heard somebody shout. "What does she bang like?"

For a moment his face froze in anger. Then he told himself he should be used to such insinuations by now.

"Ask her if there are any blow jobs going," called out another.

"How much does she charge?"

"Does she take it from behind?"

Before long they realised that he wasn't to be drawn on the subject of Caroline's sexual behaviour, and lost interest in him. A certain barrier now seemed to descend to cut him off from them. He didn't get the impression it was because he was a "Sassenach". In fact, picking out the different accents from the bar chatter, he realised that Scots made up only about half the workforce (and few of them said "och" or "havenae" instead of "haven't", for example, while the broadness of their accents varied considerably). Quite a few English voices could be heard; and the Scottish workers seemed to get on remarkably well with their cousins from south of the border. Much as they respected or at least admired MacDuggan, like everyone else on the rig, it was obvious his compatriots among the workforce thought his anti-English hangup rather silly.

Many of those present weren't British at all. Chris identified Frenchmen, Germans, Scandinavians, Dutch, Russians, Poles and a smattering of other nationalities. Colourwise there were white faces, brown faces, black faces and yellow faces, and even a man with coppery skin and straight black hair who had to be a Native American – Sioux, Chris reckoned.

There were only a couple of women in the room. One of them, he noted, was built more like a man, with a broad stocky body, heavy features and muscles like a horse's. Her hair was cut so short she was almost a skinhead. Feeling a certain disdain, he rebuked himself, since if he got to know her she might for all he knew turn out to be a very nice person. And in fact, he later deduced from what others had said that she was one of the kindest and most likeable people on the rig.

She had a loud, deep, rough voice and her language, like the men's, was peppered with four-letter words. She was talking animatedly to a couple of male colleagues, with whom she appeared totally at ease. By no means all female oilworkers were like her. But the conclusion seemed reasonable that it helped you to get on here if you were, in one way or another, one of the lads; if you talked and behaved as a man would.

No-one seemed inclined to approach him, or they were too deeply wrapped up in their own conversations. It therefore fell to him to take the initiative. He sidled up to a man who was standing at the bar waiting to be served.

"So, how long have you been working here then?"

There was a slight pause before the oilman replied. "Two years now."

"Do you like it here?"

"Aye, I guess so."

"And what do you think of all these funny…incidents?"

The man thought for a moment, and then said, "Ah really don't know."

"It's shaken things up quite a bit."

"Aye." He made no further comment.

All in all Chris could get very little out of him apart from grunted monosyllables. He couldn't decide whether he was being given the cold shoulder, or the man was naturally taciturn. Eventually he gave up. "Well, nice to talk to you." He selected another workman and made to join him.

The man saw him coming and turned to meet him, looking him straight in the eye. "I know what you are. You're a spy. A spy for the management." He had long yellowish hair, a large red face with coarse, heavy features and a thick Glaswegian accent.

"I'm just doing my job," Chris protested. Something told him it would make a better impression if he got the bit right between his teeth. "We need to know what you think about all these problems the rig's been having lately."

The Scotsman answered without hesitation. "Well it's a fucking nuisance I can tell you. You have to watch your arse all the time."

"But you want to carry on?"

"Listen, pal, this job's my life. I could transfer to another rig, of course, but I like it here on Piper. There's a good crowd here. Aren't we a good crowd, lads?" The group of friends who had gathered round him roared their agreement.

"Y'see the way I reckon, it's a hard life at the best of times. I can take it."

"Not everyone's the same, though. Some of you have decided to call it a day."

"Aye, well that's up to them." He leaned towards Barrett with a searching expression. "How do *you* fancy working here, Chris? Do you reckon you could stand it?"

"I can't see how you do," he replied. Especially after Guthrie's death and everything. "You'd have to be..."

"Crazy? Well, I suppose we are." The oilman put on a frightening expression, rolling his eyes and drawing his lips back from his teeth in a depraved leer.

"I'll bear that in mind."

The Glaswegian shook his head. "You wouldn't last here, Chris. You've got to be like us - a special breed."

"I'm sure you are," said Chris diplomatically. He resumed his questioning. "Who do you think is causing all the trouble?"

"None of the lads would, I'm sure." The man said this with just the faintest hint of doubt. "There's gotta be someone hiding somewhere."

"On the rig?"

"Nowhere fucking else that I can think of."

"The thing is, where are they hiding, and how are they managing to stay hidden?" He needed to press the point, albeit fairly gently.

"Beats me how. But it's the only answer."

"And the automation, how do you feel about that?"

"Well, we had to lose some good people. But in some ways it's better. The fewer of you there are, the more you feel part of a community. A family, I guess."

He changed the subject. "Now tell me, Chris, tell me honestly; is there anything going on between you and the lovely Miss Kent?"

"Nope," smiled Chris. "There's nothing. Nothing at all. We're just colleagues, that's all. Honestly."

"Hmm...I see. Well, Chris, there's a lot of people would say that if you're working so close with a woman like that, and you're not screwing her, you must be a pouf."

Chris realised the remark was meant to test him, and merely laughed. "I wonder if my girlfriend knows?"

The Glaswegian thumped him on the shoulder. "You're a good guy, Chris, a good guy."

He glanced at his watch. "Time for the film. Are you coming, Chris?"

"'Fraid not," answered Barrett. "I'd love to, honest, but I've got some work to do." If everyone was going to be in the cinema then there would be no opportunity to ask more questions. Instead he could do a bit of exploring, familiarising himself further with the layout of the rig and getting the feel of the place better than one could from the relatively brief tour they'd had earlier. "Another time maybe."

"OK then. See you later."

They all shook hands with him, and he went off on his rounds. He decided for the moment to just wander about, having no clear idea where in particular he should be making for.

He guessed some people would resent his snooping. But a troubleshooter ought, he reckoned, to be nosy. He had no qualms about the matter. The problem was that while he and Caroline were here people would make every effort to behave, giving a misleading impression that everything was OK. It risked rendering their task somewhat futile. But they had to take that risk.

It occurred to him that now, when everyone else was watching the film, was a good time for a saboteur to get down to business. On the other hand suspicion would be bound to fall on anyone who wasn't in the cinema at the time.

He doubled back to look in on the film, standing at the back of the room and for a couple of minutes letting his gaze travel over the audience. Was everyone here? He couldn't be sure. But the place seemed to be packed, the eyes of what must be over half the rig's population glued to the spectacle of James Bond locked in a life-or-death struggle with a villain's high-kicking henchman on board a crashing jumbo jet.

If someone was taking the opportunity to work some mischief he stood a chance of catching them in the act; but then it might be dangerous for him if he did.

A little uneasily he went on wandering; and eventually wandered into a part of the rig which had the feel of not being used much. The equipment stored there was highly specialised and used only in certain emergencies. It was here, he reasoned, that anyone who had secretly got on board Piper One, with criminal intent, would be hiding.

Be careful, he warned himself.

Suddenly he sniffed. An old familiar smell was wafting towards him. It was coming from the open door of a storage bay, and he recognised it instantly. Beer.

He stiffened. Alcohol on a rig, despite the obvious dangers of drunkenness in such an environment. Someone was being very, very stupid.

Cautiously he entered the storeroom and looked around for the source of the odour. Not immediately identifying it, he went to where it seemed to be strongest and began shifting things about. In a moment he had exposed a crate full of Newcastle Brown, with an opened bottle on the floor beside it. "Newkie Brown," he murmured affectionately.

He peered inside the crate and saw that several of the bottles had been half drunk. "Shit," he breathed. The bloody fools. They'd get the chop for this, that was for sure.

For a minute or two he hovered indecisively. It was against the drinker's code to sneak on people. He'd feel bloody awful afterwards. But if it was discovered that he knew about it and hadn't told anyone, he'd be in serious trouble. And should an intoxicated oilman fall into the sea and drown or be caught up in some lethal item of machinery it would be both his conscience and his career which suffered.

There was no-one in sight; perhaps they were hiding somewhere among all the bumf in the room. If so, it might be safer not to disturb them. Or maybe they'd heard him coming and slipped away just in time.

He turned to go, just as the door of the storage bay slammed shut and locked.

"Hey!" he shouted, running forward. He pounded on the door and yelled for several minutes before finally telling himself that whoever had shut him in would obviously not, if they were at all serious about their business, let him out of their own choosing.

This proves it, he thought grimly.

No-one else seemed to have heard, either. After a little more time had elapsed he started banging on the door again. Five, ten, fifteen minutes passed with no response.

He looked around for something to force the door with, but although he searched for some considerable time nothing suitable came to light.

He sat down on the floor and sighed wearily. He had no idea how long it would be before anyone found him.

For a while he just stared blankly at the wall. Then, gradually and a little guiltily, his thoughts and then himself turned towards the crate. He decided he didn't want to spend his time in fruitless banging and yelling when there was something more interesting he could be doing.

Just one wouldn't do any harm...

Caroline spent several hours chatting to the women, whose feelings about the state of things on Piper One were much the same as the men's. She enjoyed their company, but eventually it was time to make her way back to her room, where she would wait for Chris to join her.

Even supposing that she could feel safe in the bar, it was very much a man's world. One where, except as a sex object, she wouldn't be altogether welcome.

Almost the only woman on an oil rig, right in the middle of the bleak North Sea. The thought kept on coming back to her no matter how hard she tried to put it out of her mind.

She lay on the bed for an hour or so, scribbling down some notes for the report she would eventually make. When she'd written all she felt there was to write just then she turned to her paperback. She read another two chapters before losing interest in it.

Chris was taking a long time, she thought with irritation. She'd be glad of his company.

She decided to take a walk, boredom overcoming her reservations about going around the place on her own.

She wandered about the vast structure, looking with sharp, observant eyes for anything out of place, anything that might provide the slightest clue. Her eye fell on a ribbed metal door, and she wondered idly where it led to. On a whim more than anything else she opened it, to find herself looking out onto an observation deck.

She stepped through the door, went to the safety rail and rested her hands on it, staring down into the sea. It was a slate-grey colour and white horses were breaking out all over it.

She stood there lost in her thoughts. To be out here on her own seemed in some ways safer, isolated from possible danger. But she felt very small, very alone and very vulnerable, dwarfed by the immensity of sky and sea. Nature seemed sometimes very big and very powerful. And, she thought, it had good reason to be angry with Man right now. Its awesome hugeness made it seem ridiculous that it should put up with so much human abuse.

She told herself not to be silly; not to think of it as a living thing, with thoughts and emotions. There wasn't the slightest evidence for that.

And yet sometimes...

It was beginning to get dark, and little drops of rain were pattering on her face and on the metal of the railing. They'd said there might be a storm on the way.

She had the sudden disturbing impression that someone was standing not far away, watching her. She spun round. It was Tarrant, one of the oilmen who had greeted her on her arrival at the rig.

"Fine night."

Caroline smiled at the ironic remark. "Yes, I'll say."

"I shouldn't be out here too long," he warned.

"I won't," she replied. She resumed staring out over the sea, towards the coast of Iceland nearly a thousand miles away.

After a moment she heard Tarrant turn and move off.

Ten minutes passed; twenty, thirty. During that time it got completely dark and the weather worsened considerably. Rain lashed the deck and droplets of water splashed off the spars of the railing and formed little puddles around Caroline's feet. She could feel the structure of the rig shaking and swaying beneath her.

Deciding she wanted to be back in the cosy warmth of her room, she lingered for a moment more then turned to go.

As she did so she heard the sound of a footstep from just inside the door onto the deck. Then another.

Through the door appeared two figures in overalls and helmets; Tarrant and an oilman called McGuinness. There was a suggestion of a smile on each of their faces, but otherwise they showed no emotion as they approached her, walking in a strange, stiff fashion. There seemed to be an eerie light in their eyes.

She caught her breath, frozen in fear and horror.

The two men stopped just before her, barring her way. Spinning round, she started to run. Immediately a third figure, which must have been creeping along the deck towards her, stepped into view and planted itself solidly in front of her. She recognised an English oilman named Sam Meredith.

"What are you doing?" she snapped. "What is this?"

None of them answered. She saw Tarrant undo one of the buttons on his donkey jacket and reach inside it.

For what? A knife or a cosh?

Caroline screamed, hoping to alert someone to her danger.

Then she galvanised herself into action. Selecting her target, she lowered her head and lunged forward.

Her hard hat impacted with the pit of Tarrant's stomach, with enough force to send him staggering back, doubled up. Before he could quite recover she followed up with a sharp upward jerk of her head, the crown of the safety helmet catching him sharply on the nose. Then she turned and ran for the door while Tarrant, blood streaming from his nostrils, lurched against the safety rail. She grabbed the handle of the door and yanked it down. The door stayed firmly closed and she went cold as she realised they'd locked it. She heard the thump of heavy boots and sensed the massive figure of an oilman bearing down on her.

Whirling to face him, she whipped off her helmet and swung it round by its strap, dealing the man a vicious blow on the forehead. The rim of the helmet cut into the flesh, drawing a stripe of blood across it.

He flinched, then shot after her as she ran along the deck in search of another way of getting back inside. A trickle of blood ran into his eyes and he stopped to wipe it away.

In their determination to catch her, and hers to escape from them, everyone had forgotten the rain pouring down with increasing ferocity. Suddenly, Caroline slipped on the rain-spattered metal and went down on her backside. She struggled to get up, handicapped by her feet constantly slipping from underneath her. She felt the deck shudder as a massive body hit it; her pursuer had gone down too. Another oilman tripped over him and fell flat.

Slowly and carefully, Caroline managed to stand up. Looking round, she saw the two oilmen start to disentangle themselves from each other.

She started running again, slipped and fell. There followed a grimly comic scenario as she and her attackers struggled along, constantly falling over, getting up again, falling over.

Picking herself up for the umpteenth time, she managed to run a few yards without slipping. Then she was brought to a sudden halt as she collided with the section of solid, featureless bulkhead in which the deck ended. She regarded it in horrified dismay.

Glancing round fearfully, she saw the three oilmen moving slowly and purposefully towards her. They knew they had her now.

She screamed again, as long and as loud as her lungs could bear. "Help me, somebody! Why don't you bloody help me?"

She thought despairingly that they might not have heard her from inside, what with the pounding of the rain and the howling wind. Or maybe everyone on the rig was a psychotic rapist. They'd probably dealt with Chris already...

They came closer and closer. She pressed herself tightly against the bulkhead, feeling the metal dig into her back. In a moment or two they'd be near enough to grab her.

Tarrant was reaching into his pocket again.

The impulse came upon her in a sudden sick thrust. She dashed to her right, reaching the safety rail in just a couple of seconds, sheer speed somehow preventing her from slipping. Grabbing the topmost spar, she scrambled over the railing, twisting round so she was facing her attackers, standing with her hands grasping the rail and her feet resting on the deck for about half their length.

The men halted and glanced at each other, frowning. Her action had thrown them completely.

"If you go for me," she shouted, "uh-uh-uh-I'll jump."

She hung on to the railing for dear life, not sure she wasn't more afraid of falling than of what might happen if they got their hands on her.

If they intended to kill her, she thought, they'd simply precipitate her suicidal action, calling her bluff. If they didn't, what would they do now?

An expression something like a frown crossed Tarrant's face. Again the three men looked at one another. Then, as if reaching some joint unspoken decision, they all turned and walked away.

Tarrant produced a key and unlocked the door into the rig. They filed through it, closing it quietly behind them.

It occurred to Caroline that they might be waiting just inside the door to pounce on her as soon as she came through it. So she had to stay where she was.

If everyone on the rig was in their condition, there could be no respite for her other than capture. She had to assume they weren't. How long would her attackers wait there? Not forever, surely.

Once more she screamed for help.

No. Don't do that. If they were lying in wait, they'd know she was still there and hang about.

In any case, the wind caught her words and snatched them away.

She was terrified to move even the slightest fraction. If she slipped...

She could hear the waves crashing against the legs of the rig. If she fell into that churning sea, she was done for. There was no way any swimmer could compete against those violently tossing waves, even assuming the impact of hitting the water didn't knock her out – if not kill her. If she did survive the fall she'd either drown or be smashed against one of the legs until there wasn't much left.

She daren't look down.

The metal of the rail was wet and slippery beneath her grasp. All she could do was grip it as tightly as possible, squeezing hard until her knuckles whitened. She remained magnetised to it by sheer terror.

The wind was getting stronger. She chilled at the thought that very soon it might blow her from her place. It also seemed possible she might be dislodged by the sheer force of the relentlessly pounding rain. Or that as it got colder and colder her numbed fingers would be unable to maintain their grip.

What was beneath her? Just a dark mass of water and...

She twisted her head to one side, but couldn't make out anything in the blackness.

She was cold and wet and terrified she was going to catch pneumonia or something if this went on much longer. It was sapping her strength and willpower. She steeled herself to cling on, trying to think of things which would inspire her not to give in. There came a bellow of thunder, and then a flash of lightning lit up the rig. She jumped, and for a sickening moment thought she'd lost her grip. But she hadn't.

She tightened her hold again, bracing herself for the next flash so that it wouldn't have the same effect.

When it came it revealed, though only for a brief instant, something she hadn't noticed before. A lower deck, wider than this one, jutting out about twenty feet below it.

It wasn't directly beneath her. She'd have to work her way along the railing for about ten feet.

She relaxed her grip a little and slowly, very slowly, began to inch her way along the outside of the railing, all the time trying to keep a firm hold on it. She kept in her mind her estimate of where exactly the lower deck had been.

Don't panic. If you do you'll fall.

Thankfully, it wasn't that far to go. Once she reckoned she was right above the lower deck she drew her legs up, spreading them as wide apart as possible. Then, bracing herself, she swung herself backwards and let go of the rail.

The impact not only drove all the wind from her but sent a stab of pain all the way up her body, from the soles of her feet to the base of her skull.

She struggled upright, her feet stinging. There was a door facing her and she scrambled over and tried it only to find it was locked. She pounded on it and yelled for some minutes, but with no joy.

So she just sat down and curled herself into a tight ball against the wind and the rain and the cold.

Five

"I see," said MacDuggan, obviously shocked by what Caroline had to tell him.

After a while she had decided to have another go at attracting someone's attention, and eventually an oilman had heard the furious hammering on the door. She was soaked to the skin and her teeth were chattering. After taking a hot bath, changing her clothes and generally doing her best to smarten herself up she had gone straight to see the foreman in his office.

"Are you sure about this?" he asked.

"Of course I'm sure," she said indignantly. "You don't think I made it all up, did you?" She wouldn't put it past him.

"I'll get them all in here and see what I can do," he said slowly.

A malicious light entered his eyes. "Something *you* should know. We found your friend shut away in the store for the diving gear, pissed out of his brain over a crate of Newcastle Brown."

Caroline's eyes widened and she stared at MacDuggan in horrified amazement. "*What?*"

"Someone shut him in there," he added, seemingly as an afterthought.

"Where is he now?" she demanded.

"In his room, sobering up," said MacDuggan. He gave her the full details of the affair. When he had finished Caroline spun on her heels and marched off without a word. MacDuggan watched her go, smiling grimly and with a certain satisfaction.

Caroline knocked several times on Chris' door and on receiving no answer flung it open and stormed in. She found him lying flat on the bed, not yet quite asleep. There was no smell of alcohol; she guessed the oilmen had made him take a shower to get rid of it.

Shaking him back to something like full consciousness, she stood over him with arms folded. "Well, what have you got to say for yourself?"

"It wasn't my fault," he answered thickly, sitting up with difficulty. "Someone deliberately shut me...shut me in..."

"Maybe they did," she agreed. "But all the same..."

He grinned at her sheepishly.

"Honestly, Chris," she sighed. "It's bloody embarrassing. Oh, I'll patch it up somehow. But if you do get into trouble over it I'm not carrying the can."

"I wouldn't ask you to, Caroline."

Mollified, she patted him affectionately on the cheek. "I know you wouldn't."

"Perhaps if we can...sort this case out they'll overlook it." He lay back again, frowning as he forced his still clouded brain to think straight. "The beer could have been an attempt at more shit-stirring. Plus they might have wanted me out of the way."

"In order to get at *me.*" With pursed lips, Caroline told him all that had happened to her out on the deck.

Chris was immediately jolted back into full sobriety. Springing from the bed, he marched up to her and took her by the shoulders. "Are you all *right*?" he gasped.

"Yes, of course," she answered, though the look on his face told her he wasn't altogether convinced.

"Jesus Christ," he exclaimed, shaking his head. "Rape? Are we talking rape?"

"I don't think so," she said. "Chris, the look on their faces – the way they just stood and stared at me, and then – I don't know *what* it was. One of them started to take something from inside his coat and I thought it was a knife or a gun or something; that's when I decided it was time to beat it."

"Do you want to sleep in my room tonight?"

She nodded. She knew she could trust him not to misbehave; it was a trust based on several years of working together, of developing a mutual respect for each other not just as colleagues but as people.

"I'm not going to bed just yet," she told him. "I want this thing dealt with as soon as possible. I've already reported it to MacDuggan and he's promised to take action. I don't think he believed me at first but I insisted."

She sneezed. "I hope I haven't caught something," she said with a reproving glance at him.

She studied herself in the mirror and pouted. Prolonged contact with H20 made rather a mess of blonde hair.

"And did you learn anything from the bar talk?" she asked.

"They know something's not right here but they don't know what it is. They're not very happy, but they want to keep going if possible. I must say I have to admire them. They're a...a special breed." The phrase may have been hackneyed, but the sentiment was entirely sincere.

"Do they have any theories as to who's behind it all?"

"They believe there's a saboteur on the rig. Trouble is, they each think none of the others would do such a thing. It's a small community where everyone knows and has to trust each other. All the same everyone's been watching their back, and everybody else's too.

"The way they rationalise it is by thinking there must be someone hiding somewhere, even though it's not clear how they could avoid being discovered."

Caroline nodded slowly. Folding her arms, she paced back and forth, clarifying her thoughts by speaking them out loud. "What I can't figure out is this. MacDuggan may be a bolshy bigoted little bastard, but he seems like a man who knows his stuff. He's a strict disciplinarian, and you can tell his men respect him for that. The management tolerate him despite his faults because he's so damn good at his job.

"And he says he's been keeping a closer eye on everything since the trouble started. Yet it's still going on. It doesn't make sense to me."

She noticed that Chris was smiling. "What's the matter?" she frowned.

"Well, when you say he's tolerated despite his faults...I'm thinking he's a bit like you in that respect."

For a moment Caroline looked offended. Then – gradually – a smile spread itself across her face. "We'll discuss that remark later. Now, what about the possibility they're deliberately running the rig down because they don't like the way things are? Jamie Grant didn't think so."

"It's not the impression I got in the bar."

Caroline sank wearily into a chair. "I can't see a solution to this bloody business right now."

"It's the sort of case you're in this job to solve."

"I know that."

Someone knocked on the door, and Chris opened it to reveal Jamie Grant. The oilman addressed Caroline. "Miss, if you wouldn't mind coming to the Chief's office?"

She stood up. Chris glanced at her uncertainly and she nodded assent. The two of them followed Grant out.

"The lads are all offering to look after you," he told Caroline on the way. Without a doubt the male workforce of Piper One had had their basic urges aroused by her arrival, and had made little secret of their desire to perform coitus with her. Now that someone seemed to have actually attempted to do so the reaction was one of horror and anger. They were more than a little ashamed of their earlier conduct.

Caroline wasn't reassured. "No thanks," she shuddered.

"Are you sure about what happened?" Grant asked, clearly incredulous.

"Positive," replied Caroline impatiently. After that no-one said anything until they arrived at the office.

Caroline started in alarm when she saw the three men who had attacked her standing there. She took a step or two back, and Chris squeezed her hand protectively.

Also in the room, besides themselves and Grant and MacDuggan, were several more oilmen, their eyes focused unwaveringly on her attackers, who looked bemused and uneasy.

Caroline opened the proceedings without any invitation from MacDuggan. "Well," she began. "What's your explanation?"

The men stared at her. "Er – I'm afraid we don't know what you're talking about, Miss," said Tarrant apologetically.

"Oh you don't, do you? Well I don't know what you were up to, but I'd say it counts as harrassment if not assault. I could tell from the looks on your faces it wasn't just harmless fun. You could be in very serious trouble if I decided to press charges. You might lose your jobs, or worse."

They each continued to look blank. "Let me refresh your memory." She described in detail everything that had happened a couple of hours earlier.

The trio were staring at her as if she was mad. "We still don't know what you're on about," gasped McGuinness.

"That's right," said Meredith. "We...we just don't get it. Sorry."

Caroline frowned, and a strange chill began to creep through her bloodstream as she realised their astonishment was quite genuine.

"What time did you say the attack took place?" MacDuggan asked her.

"About nine-thirty."

He turned to the three accused. "And where were you all then?"

"In my room," said McGuinness.

"Same here," said Tarrant.

"To tell you the truth, Chief, I can't remember," said Meredith wonderingly.

"You can't remember?"

"It's weird, but...but no."

Caroline gave them her famous Look, studying their faces intently. After a few moments she selected a chair and slumped into it. "Look," she sighed. "I don't know what's going on here, but it's important I find out. For the moment, I'm not going to press any charges. But I'm telling you, I didn't dream the whole business. I don't know what the explanation is but I assure you I'm going to get to the bottom of this one way or another." She inclined her sleek head, indicating they were dismissed.

"I don't think you've got a lot to stand on," said MacDuggan after they'd gone. "There are no witnesses, for a start. If anyone had seen it they'd have gone to fetch help, or had a go themselves – at helping, I mean," he added.

"I can still report it to the police." She sat brooding for a moment, then sprang to her feet. "All right Mr MacDuggan, thanks," she said crisply. "Now what are we going to do about that, er, other business?"

MacDuggan said he would instigate an enquiry the next day into how the beer had been smuggled on board the rig. She nodded briefly and with a final thankyou left the room, Chris in tow.

Again escorted by Jamie Grant, they returned to Caroline's quarters. Once there, Caroline waited a moment or two, then opened the door a fraction and peered out. Seeing no-one who might be eavesdropping, she closed the door and sat down. "After what's just happened, I don't think we can trust anyone. I saw one of those men earlier today, had a chat with him. He seemed totally normal, an ordinary decent bloke. Back there on the deck he was like some kind of...of..." She struggled to find the right word.

"They really didn't seem to understand what had happened," Chris said wonderingly. "They insisted they'd done nothing wrong. And I'm sure they really believed it. It's spooky."

"You're telling me." Caroline leaned back against the wall. "Chris, what if there's something in the food, or the water – or something given off by the oil – that's affecting people's minds? It could explain both the sabotage and what happened to me just now."

"We'd be affected too, surely?"

"Maybe it would only take effect from time to time."

"If you're right," said Chris, "it won't make any difference what we do. Even if someone were assigned here permanently to keep an eye on things it'd mess up whatever they did."

He suddenly became very worried. "Anyone here could be affected. Including MacDuggan and the other top men."

"That's why I felt we had nothing to lose by forcing the issue. Yes, you're right Chris. We're in danger as long as we stay on the rig."

"So what do we do?"

"Tomorrow morning we'll call Aberdeen and get them to send a helicopter to pick us up. But before we leave, we'll get some samples of food and drink to take back with us. It shouldn't be too difficult; we'll just save some of our breakfast. And a few litres of the oil if we can get hold of them."

"Meantime, we'll have to watch ourselves."

"And I think the rig had better be closed, if only until Southampton have analysed the samples. There might be another death, and I don't want to risk the lives of any more personnel."

There was also the oft-mentioned possibility that her presence on the rig might itself be creating a problem. Was the attack on her a symptom of that?

"And with that decided, I think I'll have a nice cup of tea. How about you?"

"Reckon I need one."

"From now on we'd better stick together, OK? Like you said, after last night there's no-one on board the rig we can trust."

The thought occurred to him, as it must have occurred to Caroline, that if they were affected too she couldn't trust him. But then he couldn't trust her either. She was right in thinking they had nothing to lose.

They'd almost finished their tea when there came another knock on the door. Chris went with Caroline as she answered it.

She jumped back in alarm, Barrett stiffening beside her. McGuinness was standing there. They realised he was on his own, and relaxed a little.

"Could I have a word with you, Miss?" he asked quietly. His voice had a soft Highland lilt to it.

"What is it?" she asked.

His eyes flickered to Chris. "I'm sure he'll keep it confidential," Caroline said.

"Aye, that's all right then." The oilman's manner was meek, nervous, totally submissive. As before, it was difficult to believe he could have had anything to do with the disturbing experience to which Caroline had been subjected.

She gave a brief nod, and stepped back to let him enter. He didn't sit down but stood looking at her, his safety helmet dangling from his hand by its strap.

"I'm sorry to bother you, but I'd like to know where I stand. Over what you say happened on the deck. You said you wouldn't do anything for the moment...well, as you can guess I'm a little worried about things."

She thought over the matter. It occurred to her she really ought to have come to a decision earlier. The look on McGuinness' face made clear the stress he'd been under.

"All right," she said gently, nodding. "Let's say I'm not going to tell the police. I don't think it would achieve anything." She sighed. "There's something very weird going on here, that's for certain, but I don't think you meant to do what you did. No, you needn't worry about it."

He breathed out with heartfelt relief, the weight visibly lifting from him. "Thanks, Miss," he gasped. "I appreciate that."

"You're welcome."

With a friendly nod to them both he left.

"I think it's time for bed," Chris yawned.

In deference to each other's sensibilities, neither of them undressed before going to sleep, although each knew the other wouldn't be provoked to act inappropriately. Chris planted himself on the floor close to the door. He wondered briefly if he should station himself in the corridor instead, like a mediaeval retainer watching over the bedchamber of their monarch. The thought made him chuckle inwardly. Is that what I am to her, he mused.

He stayed awake, his eyes continually flickering towards the door, while on the bed Caroline, lying on one side with arms folded, let herself sink gradually into oblivion.

The ship had perfectly adequate navigational equipment, but you couldn't exactly miss Piper One in the dark. It was lit up like a Christmas tree by its warning lights and the glow from the flame of the gas burner. It looked like a city did at night, a city relocated out to sea, which in a sense it was even if its population had been much reduced from in the past.

They dropped anchor just outside the exclusion zone, and proceeded to discharge their cargo.

Ostensibly a research vessel, the four-person mini-submarine had been obtained from the former Soviet Navy, which had developed it during the Cold War, through a Lebanese arms dealer. Although somewhat adapted, it could still be used for its original purpose.

For a while it had seemed the storm might wreck the terrorists' plans. But Dave reckoned it would pass over before long, and he was proved right.

Once released from the sling in which it had been lowered from the ship by crane, the little sub moved smoothly through the now becalmed waters towards the rig. The pilot brought it right up to one of the legs and Charlotte, Dave, Kenny and Sean, clad in their wetsuits, scrambled through the hatch in its side and into the water. They swam the short distance between the sub and the rig with little difficulty, though Sean was hampered slightly by the bag of explosives attached to his belt. Charlotte reached up and grasped the metal ladder bolted to the leg. She started to clamber up it, the others following close behind. Each of the party was dressed entirely in black; perfect night-time camouflage, of course. As well as the wetsuits they had donned balaclava masks with holes cut in them for eyes, nose and mouth. Each carried an Armalite rifle, which had been contained in a waterproof case strapped to their back.

It was possible they could plant the explosives and depart without being spotted, but none of them was prepared to risk it. They had to take over the rig, and that meant finding hostages.

They scrambled through the hatch at the top of the ladder, all the time careful not to make the slightest sound. Sean had instructed them well in the art of stealth.

Charlotte radioed the submarine's operator. "Right, we're on board. You can take her back now."

Glancing down through the hatch, they saw the sub head off towards the mother ship. It wouldn't return, for their departure from Piper One was to be by helicopter.

The foursome set off in search of their objective, taking care to keep close together.

Altogether neither Chris nor Caroline slept much, the one because he was on his guard, the other because of general nerves. What little slumber they did get was abruptly cut short by a strident pinging from the rig's PA system.

Slowly they sat up, rubbing their eyes. "That's the fire alarm," Chris shouted as full consciousness returned.

He flung open the door and they hurried down the corridor towards the stairs leading up to the helipad. The same thought was in both their minds. It wasn't likely this was just a test, not at such a time of the morning. If there was a real fire, was it one more case of sabotage?

They became aware of other figures running with them. A few were in dressing gown and pyjamas, but most had donned their work clothes. It would be chilly standing about outside.

Creeping along an outer corridor, the four terrorists heard the blaring note of the alarm and froze, exchanging glances.

"Shit, what the fuck's going on?" gasped Sean. "Do you think they know we're here?"

Charlotte's face twisted with rage behind her balaclava. This was entirely unexpected. "I dunno, I dunno!" she gabbled.

They could hear the sound of running feet several corridors away.

"A fire alarm," said Kenny. "It could be a fire alarm."

Charlotte thought fast. Her head jerked up decisively. "We've come too far to give it up now. Now listen. Even if this is just a fire alarm, it could still mess up the whole operation. I think the best thing to do is to hide somewhere until things have calmed down. Then we'll make our move."

And what if it's a real fire? thought Kenny. Do we stay put until we get barbecued? But Charlotte told them they'd find out eventually if it was, as if logically that made any difference. As always, there was no arguing with her.

Within a few minutes the workforce of Piper One had gathered on the upper deck near the helipad, beneath the floodlights which illuminated it after dark. Briskly, MacDuggan issued a series of instructions to Jamie Grant and two other oilmen, then produced a clipboard and began calling out names in his powerful booming voice. His surly moroseness had entirely evaporated; now he was the Boss, professionally concerned for the safety of all those on the rig.

Five names did not answer. They were Tarrant, McGuinness, Patterson, McBeath, Arnold and Ross.

They waited for some minutes, long enough for the absent men to have reached the muster point from wherever they might have started off. But there was no sign of them. A ripple of unease ran through the crowd on the deck.

"Where the bloody hell are they?" MacDuggan bellowed. "It's McBeath's job to organise these bloody things. Why isn't he here?"

He selected four men. "Rory, Doug, Bob, Jimmy, you go and search the rig. I want to know just what's happened to those fellas. Be careful."

"I'm afraid we'll have to stay out here until they've made sure everything's safe," he told Chris and Caroline.

Caroline sat down on a spare oil drum, and Chris dropped to his haunches beside her. "I don't like this," he whispered.

She nodded. "The sooner we're away from here, the better." Her voice sounded strained.

Bob had meticulously combed just about all of C Deck in his search for his missing colleagues. There was only one place he hadn't yet looked, and that was the men's locker room, where their workclothes were kept when not needed.

He went in and turned on the light. No-one there, unless they were hiding inside one of the lockers, which he thought unlikely. His eye fell on the door to a small storeroom where various odds and ends were kept in case anyone should one day find they needed them. It was itself little more than a large locker, and he couldn't see what reason someone might have to be in there.

He hesitated, then on a whim went to the door and opened it.

The muzzle of a rifle was thrust against his chest. A harsh voice informed him that he would be killed if he made the slightest move, or words to that effect.

Six

"Would it really be a drill, at this hour?" said Caroline, cross at having had her sleep so rudely interrupted.

"I wouldn't put it past the chief," an oilman said. "He likes to keep us on our toes. I mean, a fire could start at any time. We have to be able to respond right away."

After a long period of tense, unhappy waiting three out of the four searchers returned. As soon as they caught sight of the men's faces, everyone knew something was wrong.

McDuggan and the three men withdrew into a corner to confer in agitated whispers. A little indignantly, Caroline marched up to them. "If this is something important, I think I should be in on it, don't you?" MacDuggan gave her a dirty look.

Brushing roughly past her, he addressed the assembled workers. "Right, lads. It's not good, I'm afraid. There's no fire. But there's no sign of the others – Bob's still searching C Deck. And someone's wrecked the radio, the helicopter, and the lifeboats."

A long silence followed while everyone absorbed this news, and its implications.

"But we can't be completely cut off from the mainland," said Caroline. "Everyone's got mobile phones, surely. Mine's in my room, but – "

MacDuggan took his mobile from his pocket and made the call. Or rather, tried to. After a moment he put the phone away, frowning. "I can't get through. Something's jamming the signal."

Chris tried his. He got a weird burbling sound like something from a science fiction film. "Hear that? Beats me how it's being done. I just dunno what to make of this."

At least they could boil things down a little. The saboteurs must be the five men who were absent. That was how it seemed to Chris and Caroline, anyway. While most of the workforce was gathered on the deck for the roll-call, they had smashed the various items of equipment. A couple of men had arrived at the roll-call late, but they wouldn't have had time to do the job.

"Something's happened to those five," Caroline said, "and it must have happened for a reason. The same reason we've been cut off."

"Do you think they could have done it themselves?" someone asked, hesitantly.

"If they were, they couldn't have got off the rig, not if they'd sabotaged the lifeboats and the chopper," said Doug. "Unless they just jumped into the sea."

Chris decided it was time to advance his and Caroline's theory. "I think where all this sabotage is concerned we're dealing with some drug or other that affects the mind, makes people do what they normally wouldn't. It could have made them kill themselves."

The oilmen found the idea both uncomfortable and implausible. Rory stared at Chris, then shook his head firmly. "It's more likely they caught the saboteurs in the act and paid the price."

"Seeing as they *have* disappeared, I'd be inclined to say they did it," Caroline asserted. "Maybe not all of them."

"Don't forget, Bob's still looking," Jimmy reminded them. "He may turn up something."

"The fire alarm was probably sounded deliberately," said Caroline. "To provide cover while they, or somebody, did their stuff."

"That'd mean McBeath was definitely in on it."

"Not necessarily." MacDuggan was clearly offended at Chris' suggestion. "Everyone knows where it is. Anyone could have gone along and done it."

A thought seemed to occur to him. "Just a minute," he said, leaning towards Chris and Caroline with a look of pleasurable malice. "Just a minute. You said there could be something round here which is making people bugger up the rig. Well, couldn't it have got you two as well?"

"Well all right, so it could," said Caroline. "But we couldn't have done *this*. We were with you all the time, right from when we heard the alarm."

MacDuggan grunted absently, disappointed that he couldn't implicate them.

"And I should point out," Caroline continued, "that it all started before we came on board. This thing could have affected us too, yes, but we weren't responsible for it in the first place."

Contradicted, MacDuggan found an excuse to distract attention from it. "We'd better all stick together for the time being. Stay where we can see each other."

"What about production?" Chris asked.

"It should carry on quite happily without us. We're partly automated, remember. If there are any hitches we'll sort them out as and when we can."

"And we've got to wait four days for the relief helicopter?"

"Not that long. There are routine calls made every day. When Aberdeen fail to raise us they're bound to send someone out. Probably armed police, bearing in mind what's been going on here."

"Which means," said Chris, "that whatever their plan is, whoever's behind all this is going to have to move fast. We're in big trouble."

It was then that Bob came out onto the deck with the four black-clad terrorists right behind him, Sean's rifle trained on his back.

MacDuggan swung round in outraged astonishment. "What the fucking hell is this?"

Charlotte's voice lashed out. "All of you stay exactly where you are. If anyone makes the slightest move, this man will be killed instantly."

If this development had affected MacDuggan's composure, he soon recovered it. "All right, if you say so. But is it possible you could tell me just what's going on here? Who the hell are you?"

"We are the Children of Gaia. We're out to put a stop to all the damage companies like yours are doing to this planet."

"I see," said MacDuggan drily.

"This rig is to be destroyed. But don't worry, you won't be harmed. We're going to set you adrift in the lifeboats and then tell the authorities what's happened. I expect you'll be rescued before long."

A stony silence fell over the oilmen. "Excuse me," said MacDuggan, "but I think there's something you should know."

"What?" demanded Charlotte.

He explained the situation to her.

She stared at him. It seemed to her unlikely that two sets of saboteurs should turn up in the same place at the same time. But then MacDuggan must know it was. That meant it was unlikely he was merely spinning a yarn, in order to gain time in which to find some way of turning the tables on them.

"Go and see for yourself," he suggested.

Kenny went to examine the helicopter, returning about five minutes later. "Someone's ripped out the instrument panel. They must be telling the truth."

Charlotte absorbed the development and dismissed it as of no concern. Evidently the oilmen had searched the rig, and not found any indication of the presence of another terrorist group there. If there had been such a group, intent on sabotage, they had come, done their job and gone. They were no longer a danger.

There was, however, another problem which still remained.

Kenny sidled up to Charlotte and whispered in her ear. "Our chopper is too small to take all of them. Look, if there's no way they can get off the rig we can't – "

She shook her heard fiercely, scowling, as in "just shut up will you, I'll think of something." Kenny withdrew, the anxious look on his face clearly visible to the onlooking oil workers.

Chris and Caroline exchanged glances.

The clattering sound of helicopter rotors entered earshot. Everyone looked round to see a red light appear in the distance. "Must be their pick-up," Chris whispered.

Charlotte turned to Sean. "Go and do it," she ordered.

"Wait, Sean." Kenny moved over to Charlotte, and again bent to mutter into her ear. "If you set off those bombs you'll kill them all. Fire's a certainty. With no way of getting off the rig they'll have had it."

"I know that," she hissed, irritated by the difficulty of keeping an eye on the rig personnel while paying attention to her three colleagues at the same time.

"Don't worry, Kenny, it'll be all right."

He couldn't see how. "Look, let's just plant *some* of the bombs. Enough to put the place out of action for a while."

"No, Kenny. It's got to be something really big, really spectacular. That's the only way people can be made to sit up and take notice of us. Why else have we been putting so much into this job?"

They would never kill if it could be avoided; there just wasn't any point. But the fact that they were prepared to contemplate causing chaos, destruction and even death on a large scale, if it were ultimately necessary for their purposes, meant that they were *doing* things. They had passed a certain point. They had achieved something, namely the creation of a totally new force in world politics. This was history, and it was they who were making it.

The thrill she felt at the thought was fantastic. They would erupt onto the world's stage the way Palestinian terrorism had done at the 1972 Olympics.

They'd come too far to give it up now.

"We can't do it, Charlotte," Kenny repeated, his voice rising in agitation. "You promised me no-one would be harmed. If anybody..."

"Keep your voice down, you stupid arsehole!" she snarled, her teeth grinding together savagely. She shot a glance at Bob; had he overheard what they had been saying?

She muttered an order to Sean. Shouldering his rifle, he grabbed Bob by the arm and dragged him over to his colleagues. A powerful shove in the back sent him staggering into them. Sean backed away, his rifle pointed at the oilmen, to rejoin the other terrorists, who likewise kept their guns trained on the group of workers.

Charlotte nodded to Sean. "Go ahead." He hurried off with the bag, Kenny staring after him helplessly.

"Did you find any trace of the missing men?" Rory asked Bob.

Bob shook his head. "No. And I'd searched just about everywhere."

"I'm more concerned about what this bunch are going to do," said Caroline, glancing for the umpteenth time at the four terrorists.

The oilmen began muttering uneasily among themselves. The frenzied whispering, certain words their ears had picked up, the obvious agitation of the terrorists, and the general vibrations being sent out from the four had unsettled them.

As much to pass the time as for any other reason, Caroline studied the terrorists, trying to size them up, to understand the motivation behind what they were doing. She thought the woman looked familiar; not her face, which was masked by the balaclava, but her voice, along with her general manner and body language. And once she seemed to be staring at Caroline, as if trying to decide whether she'd seen her before.

While Sean was off planting the bombs, Charlotte had intended to use the time to think of some solution to the problem. None had occurred to her.

She couldn't keep the helicopter hanging around forever.

MacDuggan decided it was time to assert his authority. He shouldered his way to the front of the group, the workmen respectfully moving aside for him. Determined not to be outdone, Caroline followed.

"Excuse me," MacDuggan said forthrightly, "but may I ask what exactly you're intending to do?"

Charlotte knew that if she hesitated in the slightest before replying, it would increase the workers' suspicions. "Just plant one or two bombs, that's all. Enough to put the rig out of action for a bit. You should be all right as long as you stay where you are."

Caroline thought the look on the woman's face, indeed everything they'd seen and heard, was all wrong. Her unease communicated itself to the others on the deck.

That other terrorist, the one with the bag, had been gone a long time.

Just one or two places, they'd said.

The air was like thin, brittle glass.

Sean reappeared, the bag dangling limply from his hand, obviously empty now.

Charlotte took her radio from the pocket of her wetsuit and they saw her speak into it. The hovering helicopter started to descend towards the rig. It touched the surface of the helipad and settled.

Charlotte lifted her rifle. "Get back!" she shouted to the oilmen.

It was the miserable, and also horrified look on Kenny's face as he, Dave and Sean turned and walked towards the helicopter, while Charlotte backed away with her Armalite covering the oilmen, that finally confirmed their suspicions.

In a moment, they'd lose any chance of acting to save themselves. Suddenly, panic overcame them and they surged forward, attempting to rush the terrorists. Chris saw Caroline go flying, her safety helmet coming off and her hair tumbling free, as a couple of men cannoned into her. He flung herself on top of her, afraid she would be trampled. Charlotte began blazing away with the rifle, the muzzle of the weapon sweeping round in a deadly arc. Men and women twisted and fell dying as she sprayed them with bullets. Among them Chris thought he saw the Glaswegian and the Sioux. Sean and Dave joined in while Kenny cowered back against the safety railing in horror. Fear of instant death overriding any other thought, the surviving workers ran off, seeking cover inside the superstructure of the rig.

As Sean turned toward his three companions, he felt an arm wrap tightly around his neck. He just had time to register that one of the workmen had managed to get behind them before there was a kind of explosion of light, brilliant blinding light, just in front of his eyes. It seemed to pierce right through them into his brain and fill it with an intense searing pain.

Charlotte turned from cutting down two more oilmen and looked round for her companions. She froze in sheer amazement at what she saw.

They were all pointing their rifles at her, their faces transformed into impassive zombie-like masks. MacDuggan and four other oilmen were standing close by, regarding her in the same emotionless, inhuman way.

"Throw down your weapon," ordered MacDuggan. His voice was a harsh, Dalek-like rasp.

In a trance-like state of astonishment, Charlotte relaxed her grip on the rifle, letting it slip from her fingers. One of the oilmen came forward and took the weapon, covering her with it. Caroline Kent and Chris Barrett were wriggling out from beneath a pile of dead bodies, coughing and gasping for breath. Slightly stunned, Caroline staggered to her feet. She reeled about dazedly, face bright red. Chris thumped her between the shoulder blades as hard as he could. She was silent for a moment, then began to draw in air in great wheezing gulps. Gradually her colour returned to normal.

"All right?" he asked. Her nose was bleeding and there was an ugly purple bruise on her forehead where an oilman's boot had kicked it.

"Yes, thanks," she replied. She took in the scene. "What the hell is going *on*?"

MacDuggan motioned for Charlotte to stand with Chris and Caroline. "Check they are all dead," he told the oilman who had been covering her, gesturing towards the bodies which lay scattered about the deck. The man proceeded to turn over each one with his foot, checking for signs of life.

The sound of rotors made everyone look up. The chopper was rising slowly into the air. The four oilmen watched it swing round and head out over the sea, their faces betraying no emotion, no concern.

"What's happening?" Caroline asked MacDuggan. "Are we supposed to be prisoners?"

"All will be explained to you soon," MacDuggan answered. All trace of an accent was gone from his voice. It was flat, hollow, toneless. As he spoke, a trickle of saliva emerged from the corner of his mouth and ran down his chin.

Caroline noted that the look on the oilmen's faces was identical to that of the three who had attacked her earlier. "I think we're about to find out one or two things," she told Chris.

They heard the sound of a rifle shot and looked at each other in anguish and horror.

"Let us go to the supervisor's office," MacDuggan said as the fourth oilman rejoined the group. "Bring the prisoners."

"There you are," Chris muttered.

When they reached the office, MacDuggan stood thinking intently for about a minute before reaching forward and flicking on the intercom built into his desk.

Out of sight behind one of the structures on the deck, the little group of surviving oilmen stood conferring. "I can't work out what it means," said Rory. He described what he'd seen on peering out from behind a row of oildrums. "The boss and several of the lads seemed to be in cahoots with them."

"I reckon we should stay here," said Jimmy. "Wait till the police come and let them sort it out." This met with a murmur of agreement.

Then they heard the crackle of static that preceded a tannoy announcement, and MacDuggan's voice boomed out. "This is the rig superintendent speaking. The situation is under control. Please will all personnel come to my office where I shall explain what is happening."

"What d'you reckon?" asked Doug.

Jimmy frowned. "I dunno. Was that MacDuggan? He didn't sound right to me."

"Nor me," said a third oilman.

"Yeah, I think we'd better play safe. Find somewhere to hide until the police come. There's been enough funny business going on here lately."

The helicopter was now hovering a hundred feet above the surface of the sea, a mile or two from the rig, while the pilot and co-pilot held an urgent conference.

"Did you see what happened?"

"Yeah, the rig crew have taken over. I know this sounds crazy but I swear that Kenny and Dave and Sean had their guns on Charlotte."

The other frowned. "Maybe they got cold feet about the whole thing," he suggested, searching for an explanation.

"Kenny might. But not the others. And even if Kenny had I don't see him having the guts to go *that* far."

"Maybe they've been double-crossing us. Maybe they're spies for the police."

"Or they could have thought things would go better for them if they shopped us. Christ, if they tell everything..."

"Well, whatever's happened we can't go back. They're on their own now. Let's just get back to base as fast as we can. Then we'll lie low until we hear something."

They banked, turned, and headed back towards the coast.

Seven

In the office MacDuggan stood very still while he waited for some response from the surviving oilmen, his whole body seeming rigid with tension. Nearby Charlotte, Chris and Caroline were all standing close together, the muzzles of Sean and Dave's Armalites only inches from them. Charlotte had been made to remove her mask. After a few more minutes had passed MacDuggan spoke into the intercom again. "You are all to come to my office immediately, I repeat immediately. If you are not all here within twenty minutes, we will kill the hostages. You and you alone will be responsible for their deaths."

In their hiding place, the oilmen shifted uncomfortably. "Shall we give them the benefit of the doubt?" asked one.

"I think we should, if there's lives at stake," said Jamie Grant.

"I'm staying right where I am," declared Don Connell, a big, mean-looking, bearded man.

"He said he wanted all of us there. It's no good otherwise."

"Then we may as well stay where we are. You can go if you want to but I'm not walking into the bloody lions' den. We've no knowing what'll happen if we go into that office. Aye, there's lives at stake. But if we do what he says there could be more. And they'll be ours."

Several of the men made to get up, then changed their minds and slumped back.

They waited while the last few minutes ticked away. Those who had wanted to give themselves up sat with their heads bowed, looking miserable and sickened, while the others stared impassively at the wall.

Chris and Caroline hardly dared look at their watches. Standing beside his colleague, Chris could feel her stiffen, sense the fear emanating from her. He tensed his muscular body, ready to make a fight of it if he could. Charlotte seemed calmer, although her eyes kept darting about as if seeking something she might use to get out of their predicament.

Caroline swallowed. "Please. Tell us exactly what it is you're after. If you're going to kill us, I think I'd at least like to know why."

None of their captors answered her.

They found all sense of time had gone. This might have been a relief, but it wasn't, because it meant every moment could be their last. How many minutes had passed now? Ten? Fifteen?

Caroline was trying to look grimly composed, to be the ice maiden. Despite all her efforts, a little whimper of fear escaped her. Chris wanted to make some comforting gesture but was afraid in case any movement on his part resulted in instant death.

Would she crack up, or retain her composure until the last? For that matter, would he?

There was manifestly no sign of Grant and the others.

They saw MacDuggan look at his watch. Then he turned to one of the oilmen. "Fetch some rope. Hurry, but be careful. The humans who remain at large are a threat to the plan." He had decided it was safer not to leave the office unless absolutely necessary.

Caroline and Chris swayed giddily, gasping in relief. Whatever he was planning, it didn't look as if MacDuggan was going to carry out his threat to kill them. Otherwise, he'd simply shoot them there and then. It looked like they were safe, for the time being anyhow.

The foreman's attention now seemed to focus on Charlotte. His subordinates too were glancing in her direction, though despite the distraction neither Chris nor Caroline felt like taking any risks. "Who are you and who are you working for?" MacDuggan demanded.

The presence of the guns suggested to Charlotte it would be best to co-operate. "I'm Charlotte Straker and I'm a member of the Children of Gaia. We're dedicated to protecting the Earth and its living things from all the evils of pollution and the industrial society."

"Hey, I've just remembered where I've seen you before," piped up Caroline. "At that business in Madrid. You were one of the protestors, weren't you?" Her tone hardened. "You threw a pot of paint over me." She wasn't likely to forget the incident; her hair had been absolutely ruined.

"Did I? Good." Charlotte eyed her in a rather unsettling fashion. "I've just remembered who *you* are; Caroline Kent. You're on our files."

Caroline felt rather chuffed at the thought. "As an evil agent of international capitalism, no doubt."

"Yes," hissed Charlotte. "You are."

"Come to think of it, it's not the only time our paths have crossed, is it?" They had first encountered one another in Stockholm, where the world's leading oil companies had agreed to meet to discuss matters of concern to them all, such as the then level of oil prices and the ways and means of reducing the pollution their activities were causing. Caroline had been a member of the delegation sent by International Petroleum.

The group Charlotte then belonged to, and which later amalgamated with several others to form the Children of Gaia, had been unimpressed by the companies' professed commitment to change, even though they were clearly making a serious effort to address the issue. They had gone to protest, standing outside the building where the conference was taking place, chanting slogans, brandishing placards and attempting aggressively to engage the delegates in conversation as they arrived, prefacing their words with "Excuse me, I want to know how you think you can justify..." or "I want to ask you something. Did you know that..."

Caroline alighted from her taxi to find herself confronted by a group of chanting protestors. Seizing on her, Charlotte pushed her way to the front and stood firmly before her, barring her way.

She described in graphic detail the effects of oil pollution upon the natural environment, demanding to know what Caroline intended to do about it and whether she thought there wasn't a contradiction between any claim on her part to be concerned about the problem and her position as an employee of one of the world's major polluting agents.

Caroline replied politely and sincerely that the environment was an important issue which sorely needed to be resolved, and that she believed this was best done in a way which preserved the free market (she couldn't really have said otherwise without her bosses noticing). Although the big decisions weren't down to her alone, she would play her part in the matter, and do all she possibly could to find non-polluting ways of producing energy. Charlotte, not inclined to be fobbed off with such obvious window-dressing, treated her to a fierce (and somewhat rambling) diatribe on the evils of globalisation and her own complicity in them.

She had already begun to conceive a strong dislike for Caroline. The smart, expensive clothes and the brisk, authoritative tone of voice irritated her. Now, on top of that, there was the fact that she withstood the barrage of invective imperturbably, smiling politely at everything Charlotte said and from time to time affecting a look of fascinated interest, or nodding vigorously in agreement. All the time Charlotte had the infuriating impression that the woman wasn't really listening to her.

Getting angrier, she had thrust her face into Caroline's and, raising her voice several more decibels, begun belabouring her in a manner which amounted to personal abuse. Eventually she had given up and turned away in disgust, shouting out one last insult. Treating her to a final friendly smile Caroline walked on into the building, entirely unruffled.

Subsequently Fate, with its usual perversity, seemed to conspire to bring together two forceful personalities with very different ways of doing things, who were bound to generate enmity between themselves. The episode with the pot of paint had already been mentioned.

The Stockholm conference having not quite succeeded in achieving its objectives, a further meeting was held in New York. The protests got out of hand when some people started throwing bottles at the delegates, and clashes resulted with the police. After the incident an interview took place on TV, live from just outside the conference building, between a representative from the company and one of the protestors. It had been agreed that the latter's wish to remain anonymous should be respected, otherwise they probably would not have consented to do the interview. Accordingly, they came with a towel wrapped around their head.

Caroline had managed to wangle it so that she got to speak for IPL; it had been discovered that she looked good and performed well on television. As luck would have it, the spokesperson for the protestors was Charlotte.

Everything went ahead fairly peacefully until the interviewer referred to the fact that a number of policemen had been injured, one or two quite nastily. Charlotte declared she had no sympathy for them, since they too were totalitarian oppressors, doing the work of the governments who allowed and indeed encouraged the pollution.

The temperature in Caroline's vicinity suddenly dropped. Though she kept her voice calm and reasonable, her opinion of what Charlotte had said was clear.

She felt a sort of outraged puzzlement. "But they're only doing their job. They'd protect any other kind of meeting if they were told to, yours included. Why's your quarrel with them too?"

"They're not part of the solution so they're part of the problem." Charlotte shrugged her shoulders, as if the truth of what she said was obvious and no further comment was needed. "They could choose a different career if they wanted to."

"Someone's got to do it," Caroline said. "It might as well be them."

Charlotte didn't seem in the least impressed by her logic. "They have a choice. They choose to support oppression. There's no excuse; everyone knows what's going on."

"So you don't apologise for what you did to those policemen?" asked the interviewer.

"No, of course not. They're Fascists."

Suddenly Caroline could stand it no longer. Before the gaze of the astonished interviewer, and millions of television viewers throughout the world, she hurled herself at Charlotte, grabbed the towel and pulled. Charlotte was so taken aback that at first she didn't react. Then, her face showing horror as the towel came away, she ran out of the camera's field, making desperate attempts to hide her features while still being able to see where she was going. Caroline grabbed her and swung her round to face the camera again. She tried to break free and the two of them fell to the ground fighting like cats. After a moment Charlotte gave up the struggle and ran off, concentrating on protecting her identity. Two of her fellow travellers grabbed her and bundled her away, her hands clasped tightly to her face.

The interviewer turned to address his audience. "Well, you saw it here on ABTV."

Caroline had been given a severe talking-to by her superiors after the incident, and they'd slapped a ban on her appearing on TV for a while, much to her chagrin. But it had been worth it just to see the look on Charlotte's face. And the police and intelligence services of all the leading Western nations, including the FBI and CIA, had identified her as a wanted criminal, with the result that she was now condemned to life on the run, with all the stress and inconvenience such an existence entailed.

"How lovely it is to see you again," said Charlotte, in a voice which sent a shiver down Chris' spine.

"Yes, isn't it?" said Caroline brightly.

"Be silent!" commanded MacDuggan, obviously angry at these distractions from the matter in hand. He turned back to Charlotte. "Continue. You were intending to destroy this installation, were you not?" The effect of the precise, oddly stilted tones was unsettling.

"We thought it was time people like us had an impact. Blowing up an oil rig would be the start. We chose this one because of all the pollution it was causing."

MacDuggan's response caused Charlotte to sit up sharply in surprise. "Your organisation is no longer needed," he said. "We are about to achieve your aims for you."

Her eyes widened. "How? Who...who *are* you?"

"This will...explain better than...than I could." MacDuggan's voice had begun to sound hoarse and strained, the words slightly slurred.

He reached inside his overcoat and after a moment's fumbling took something out. It was a chunk of some crystalline substance, silver-white in colour and shaped rather like the pincer of a crab.

MacDuggan stared intently into its glittering surface, his lips working silently. They had some idea he was receiving instructions from it; or giving them. Then he offered it to Charlotte, who took it curiously.

"Place it against your forehead," he instructed. She obeyed.

After a moment, her face took on an expression of trance-like wonder. Her eyes widened and began to shine like those of a religious zealot who thought they were witnessing the Second Coming.

She remained in that state for some minutes. During that time his subordinate returned with several coils of thick rope and proceeded to bind Chris and Caroline securely to two of the chairs in the office. Once that task was accomplished MacDuggan posted Sean as a guard just outside the door, rifle in hand, and instructed Kenny and one of the oilmen to search the rig for the other remaining personnel and kill them.

Charlotte took the crystal from her forehead and handed it back to MacDuggan. She sat down slowly with the look of a person overwhelmed by some profound, intoxicating revelation.

"Well, what did it say?" asked Caroline flatly.

Charlotte spoke slowly, wonderingly, occasionally seeming to struggle to find the words with which to express her thoughts. "They're aliens...in a sense. They were on this planet before us...an intelligent species. Insects...or something like it. They did most of the things we've done, colonised every part of the Earth. But not space. They were more concerned with this world, with exploring its secrets and protecting its ecology. They had a much better relationship with the environment than we do. They lived in harmony with the Earth, developed a technology that worked with it and didn't pollute it. They're wonderful creatures.

"One day...an asteroid. Same as what they think happened with the dinosaurs. Most of them were wiped out. A very few survived, but they couldn't continue to exist as physical beings, not in large numbers. The climate change caused by the meteorite, the ecological disruption, made that impossible. So they found a way to transfer their minds directly into those things." She nodded towards the crystal. "One or two of them kept their physical bodies and put themselves into suspended animation in some place under the sea bed. They slept for millions of years, the guardians of the crystal. A machine was programmed to wake them up if anyone entered the chamber where it was kept, in case that person might damage or steal the crystal. They were hoping that by the time they revived the Earth would be habitable for their kind again.

"They're angry at the mess we've made of "their" world – they can't help continuing to think of it as theirs. Otherwise they might not mind us too much. It's a bit like the way you feel when you have to move, to leave a home where you were happy, and then see the new owners letting it go to seed."

It was some time before either Caroline or Chris could speak. On their travels around the world on assignments for their company they had seen many strange things. But the tale Charlotte had to tell affected them in a way neither of them could have described in words.

"After they woke up again," Caroline said, "what happened?"

"Then they made contact with MacDuggan. He was working alone on one of the rigs."

They imagined that dark, brooding personality, alone on the rig with his thoughts and his memories. He had cut himself off completely from human company, by his own wish. Occasionally he might go out on deck, to stare moodily across the sea. And while he was there, so isolated, so remote from any other human person, utterly absorbed into himself, the aliens had come.

"Through him they learned about your company. About all the damage it was doing to our planet. Who its top people were."

She turned to look at Caroline. "And about you. Young, enthusiastic, intelligent. Just the sort of person IPL wanted. Ambitious, self-motivated, hard-working, assertive. The queen bee, one might say.

That's how they think of you; they're insects, after all. And so good at your job you were already head of a major department at twenty-five. Even by Human Resources standards, it was a meteoric rise. They could see what was going to happen. They knew that in five, ten, maybe fifteen, years' time – but no later than that – you'd be head of the company."

The others saw Caroline start, her body straining at its bonds. A warm, electric thrill, a glow of pride and emotion, spread through her.

"Oh," she gasped. "Uh-uh-uh-oh."

"Head of a multinational corporation employing millions of people in thirty countries. An organisation which controlled the flow of oil, the supply of one of the world's most vital resources. And as a result, had considerable economic and political clout. An international empire as powerful in its own way as any there's ever been. A force that could unmake kings, presidents, prime ministers, decide the fate of nations."

Caroline was in a state of euphoria, her eyes wide and shining. She stared at Charlotte, not quite believing despite her unshakeable confidence in her own abilities that what she had just been told could be true. Chris felt a sudden surge of tenderness towards her.

"You were vital to their plans. They thought that if they could control you, they could control the company. You'd close it down and there'd be no more pollution. That's why they started all the trouble here; they knew you'd be sent out to deal with it. They knew you couldn't resist the challenge.

"It would have looked odd if any of them had come down to London, because no Piper One employee had any reason to while things were going well. And in a remote, isolated place like this rig it'd be easier to do the job without anyone noticing.

"They started to take over the rig crew, one by one. It had to be done gradually, and carefully, because there were still some fifty workers on board despite all the automation.

"That crystal thing, as I said, is a repository of minds. *Their* minds. There are some hundred or so aliens existing in there as disembodied intelligences. The device has the power to transfer them into human brains and so take them over. The alien influence works subconsciously most of the time, but it can cut in whenever it needs to. After it's withdrawn into the subconscious, the person has no recollection of what they did under its control. That was useful because it helped to cause confusion.

"They tried to convert you at the start, when you were out on the deck alone. They thought that was the best chance they'd get. After the attack everyone was on their guard. And it was likely you'd clear out at the first opportunity. So they needed to cut the rig off from the mainland for a while; that'd give them more time to think up and put into action some plan for getting you alone. It would help if they could stir things up, cause a bit more confusion.

"It was easier for them to do it at night, but they weren't taking any chances. I think they must have sabotaged the helicopter before they set off the alarm. If everyone was out there on the deck, someone might have seen them do it. Then, when everyone else was at the roll-call, they got to work. One of them saw to the lifeboats, another the radio.

"So there you are. And then, of course, we came along."

"There's no need to tie me up," she said to MacDuggan. "I'm on your side. You know that, don't you? You want to stop them ruining this planet, well so do I."

The passion and conviction in her voice seemed to convince MacDuggan. Again, something like a human emotion, but not quite – a suggestion of relief – crossed his face. The tension evaporated from him.

He indicated to Dave to put his Armalite down. There was no further point in holding it on Charlotte. Then he turned towards Caroline. "Now we must do what we came here for." He got the crystal out again. The movement gave Caroline a sense of deja vu, taking her back to the struggle on the deck.

"Wait," called out Charlotte. "Do what you just did with me. Let her see what I saw. Let her feel the agony of your people. You never know, when she does she may decide to join us. We may as well give her the chance to redeem herself."

Again MacDuggan stared fixedly down at the crystal, seeming to communicate with it. He pressed it to Caroline's forehead. Through no effort on her own part a succession of vivid, evocative images flashed before her. She saw them both with her eyes and with her mind.

She saw a verdant, living world, covered in one vast sprawling carpet of green. And through that dark, primeval forest moved a huge spidery shape. She seemed to see the scenes that followed through its eyes.

Its kind multiplied a billionfold, swarming over the Earth's surface. The sky and the seas were filled with their graceful, beautiful bodies. And the mighty forests, along with the air above them, rang with the chirruping of a million insect voices talking and singing.

Scurrying about ant-like, the creatures built huge honeycombed domes filled with light; sailed through the sky on raft-like structures, or inside translucent winged shapes like planes but giving the sense of being somehow alive. Working together in total harmony, every action orchestrated and synchronised perfectly, they created fantastic and sublime works of art; buildings and machines whose purpose and functioning defied all understanding. Theirs was an ordered society, happy in its total, and willing, conformity yet prizing beauty.

She couldn't understand the strange thoughts and sensations that filled her mind, but the visions she saw were enough to communicate and arouse emotion. She could see that the creatures were happy. The sound of their voices, that soft susurrating murmur, filled the air like a universal sigh of contentment. The planet sighed with them.

Then suddenly, a vast black shape filled the sky, blotting out the sun. The insect figures milled about in alarm and confusion, their high chattering voices saturated with terror.

A rushing noise filled the air and drowned out the insect voices. Then silence.

Darkness…all-embracing darkness.

And when, after three hundred million years, the last survivors emerged from their slumber, shock and horror. The air was thick with the bitter, acrid stench of – what? It was a smell they had never experienced before, that had not been known in their time. They didn't like it. They sensed at once that it was alien, alien and *wrong*. Indeed, to them it was evil.

They saw that the Earth was dying, slowly but surely. They knew that because of their link with the planet. Its living things were sickening from the unnatural substances in the air and soil.

And they felt anger, pain, distress. Their Earth was calling out to them; calling for help.

They had to do something. Not just for their sake, but for the world's too.

They would.

MacDuggan retrieved the crystal and stepped back. Allowing the others to see the tears glistening in Caroline's eyes.

Eight

"I still say we should have done something," muttered Jamie Grant.

"Will you shut up about that, man?" growled Doug. "What *could* we have done? It's too late now, anyway."

Suddenly he stiffened, hearing the sound of a footfall. "Someone's coming."

He listened carefully, his unease growing. The footsteps were soft, stealthy ones. Made by people who didn't want anyone to know they were there.

By his reckoning there were quite a few of the crew who, unless they were among those lying dead on the deck, had run off when the terrorists opened fire and might still be wandering about the rig. Several had joined them in the past hour or so, but there had been no new arrivals for some time.

Grant peered out cautiously from their hiding place and saw Kenny and the possessed oilman stalking towards it, rifles at the ready. As he ducked back out of sight Kenny saw him and fired. The bullet spanged off the wall an inch or two from his head.

"Jesus Christ, they're coming after us!" he gasped.

"Let's get out of here!" They scrambled to their feet and ran. Briefly Grant thought of staying to try and reason with the two but something about those emotionless slab-like faces told him it'd be a waste of time. A dangerous one.

"Well," said Charlotte, "what do you think?"

Caroline was still speechless, overwhelmed by everything the crystal had shown her. They waited.

She twisted round in her chair to face MacDuggan. "I'm sorry," she said, her voice little more than a whisper. "I'm sorry, believe me."

"So what are you going to do about it then, Caroline?" Charlotte demanded.

Caroline addressed MacDuggan, or rather the being controling him. "Look, there's obviously a lot we can learn from you. If there's any way we can stop the pollution but still keep our technology, we have to try to find it. Why don't you just untie us and then we can talk some more."

MacDuggan seemed hesitant. Then Charlotte's harsh voice rasped out. "Don't trust her."

"You think she will deceive us?"

"Don't trust any capitalist. Don't trust anyone in her position. If it turns out it doesn't work, she'll be quite happy to go back to wrecking our planet just for the sake of money. Her kind are all the same. We need to use force, and to be committed to that path, that path only, right from the start. Anything else our enemies will try to exploit."

"It's not up to me alone," said Caroline. "But I'll do my best to see you get a fair hearing. I can't promise anything more."

"Then you're no good to us, Caroline. Not on your own account."

Chris had been silent for some time. Now he spoke out. "How can we be sure these...these people are all good? That their civilisation didn't have its own faults? Maybe that crystal only shows the bits they want you to see. In any case, it's different from ours. What suits them wouldn't necessarily suit us."

Caroline nodded.

"They cared for the Earth," Charlotte said. "That's all that matters." She turned sadly to MacDuggan. "I don't think it's worked."

"Then we shall take control. She will serve us whether she wishes to or not."

"She'd still know your influence was in her mind. There might be something she could do to wreck the plan."

"She would not remember what we have told her. That is a consequence of the possession." Again he was moving towards Caroline.

"Um...hold on a moment," said the troubleshooter, smiling. "I'm afraid it's not going to be as straightforward as you think."

MacDuggan hesitated, a frown crossing his brow. "What do you mean?"

"I get the impression your society was – is – highly stratified. One person, or group of people, has full responsibility for each area, each vital service. Ours isn't like that. If I was head of the company, that wouldn't mean I could stop the oil flowing just by snapping my fingers."

"You are lying," MacDuggan said.

She struggled fiercely, scowling, as he advanced on her with the crystal. Nobody, if she could possibly help it, was going to be in *her* mind telling her what to do, using her body and soul for their own ends without her consent. The thought of it angered and distressed her.

Again Charlotte stopped MacDuggan. "I'm afraid she's telling the truth." She laughed. "They're perceptive, in their own way," she told Caroline and Chris. "It's partly logic, and partly a sort of intuition. They could tell you'd be head of IPL one day, barring unexpected happenings like your going under a bus. But their logic isn't fully informed. And then there's the way their thought patterns work. They're receiving signals from the human brains they inhabit, but they don't evaluate the information the way we would. You're right, our society's very different from their own; so different that they find it very hard to understand. It works on totally...totally alien, to them, lines. What they learn they interpret according to their own customs, which may not be the same as ours. They thought that because the company was responsible for the pollution, if they eliminated or controlled the people who ran it they'd solve the problem. They're wrong, of course."

"There are many other companies which produce oil," she told MacDuggan. "Then there are the politicians, the financial institutions, the public. No-one would let her do it. They'd think something extremely strange was going on. The economy of this planet, or a very big slice of it, depends on oil. And capitalism. You've got the politicos and the big businesspeople, who decide what happens anyway.

Beneath them are the people who consume the oil; the ordinary citizen, the transport industry, the essential services. The company produces to meet people's needs, or what the people think are their needs, not just to line the pockets of those who run it. The politicians would make sure, in the last resort, that it did that job. You're up against a whole society, a whole culture. You won't destroy it by taking over just one person."

Caroline studied MacDuggan's face. It was hard to read the strange expressions that kept appearing there, but she had the impression he was convinced by Charlotte's words. He'd no reason to think she was lying, at any rate.

"So we need to take over the major world governments. If possible, the ordinary people as well. By force, if necessary. Now I'm sure there are some people in my organisation who'd be right behind us. With the powers you've got, and our support, you stand a chance."

Oh no, thought Caroline.

"Yes," breathed MacDuggan, his lips forming a kind of half-smile which said as much as a full one would on a normal human. The same look was on the faces of his subordinates. "Yes, that is how it should be," he whispered softly.

Charlotte appeared to be taking charge. "We need hostages for when the police come, as they will do before too long." She nodded at Chris and Caroline. "These two will do. When the police get here, we'll take their helicopter and I'll detonate the explosives we planted. We can start our campaign with the destruction of Piper One."

"Killing the police and any of the workers who are still alive?" Caroline snapped.

"It's necessary, I'm afraid."

"Necessary?"

"We have to cause as much devastation as possible in order to make our point. If it means people have to die, well of course I'm sorry about that. But there's simply no alternative and it's pointless to go on agonising about it.

"They probably don't see it that way, but they'll be dying in a good cause. One that's bigger than any other geopolitical issue right now; bigger than you and me, than September 11th and the War On Terror. It's a worthwhile sacrifice; right now, the best there could possibly be."

Caroline decided that someone couldn't be as pathologically callous as Charlotte unless there was some deep emotional trauma at the root of it. She studied the woman's features keenly, as if trying to search behind the face, behind the eyes, for some clue to its nature.

"I think you need help," she said.

The remark was as unwise as it was well-meant. Eyes flashing, Charlotte stepped forward and dealt her a vicious backhander.

"Leave her alone," shouted Chris, enraged.

Caroline glared up at Charlotte defiantly.

"I don't know what you're trying to prove – or hide," Chris said. "But it's pretty pathetic. And not just pathetic. If you could only see yourself right now, the way you're carrying on; it doesn't look very nice, believe me. And it proves you need to see a bloody psychiatrist."

He was trying to divert Charlotte's attention from Caroline to himself, but didn't succeed. She shot him a brief, contemptuous glance then returned her attention to his colleague.

"It's you that needs help," she snarled. "Help to see how you're destroying our planet and how you can stop it."

"Did you have a difficult childhood, by any chance?" Caroline's tone was by no means unkind.

Charlotte spat in her face. "You stuck-up capitalist bitch."

"You're in no position right now to be insolent," she went on. "If we didn't need you I'd..." She left the sentence unfinished. "No, if it's necessary for those people to die then they'll die." She indicated MacDuggan. "As for him, I don't think he's much bothered. You and your kind have given him every reason to hate you. He'll do what it takes to get our message across."

"*Our* kind?" exclaimed Chris. "You're one of us."

"I'm not sure about that," Caroline muttered.

"Oh, it's not the whole human race I hate, Caroline darling. Only those who don't take proper care of our planet."

"So what's going to happen to us eventually?" Chris asked.

"Your knowledge of the company's operations will be very useful to us."

"And after that?" he demanded.

"It'd better to use us as spies, wouldn't it?" Caroline said. "The enemy within."

"You're just trying to save your own skin," sneered Charlotte.

"Of course. Wouldn't you?"

"All the same, you're quite right. You would be more use to us as spies. So that's what you'll be. You wouldn't *know* you were being manipulated, so it needn't cause you any distress."

"Charlotte, believe me, it wouldn't work," said Caroline. She looked round at the four aliens – that was effectively what they were, right now – signifying she meant them to hear what she was about to say. "You can't go back to a pre-industrial way of life. The vast population that's grown up since then on the benefits of oil and coal and gas...you just couldn't support it. Millions of people would die. Can't you see that?"

"And if they do die? What have we ever done that's been of any benefit to this planet?" said Charlotte passionately. "We've spoilt it for too long. The world has a right to live, to breathe. To be at one with its creatures."

"We've got rights too," Chris said.

"What you want is renewable energy, yeah?" Caroline continued. "A technology that works with nature, that doesn't pollute, doesn't introduce anything unnatural into the ecosystem. And you want it now."

"Of course."

"I agree we need to invest more in renewables, try and find some way of making them work. The company's always been in favour of that. I've been in favour of it.

"But the technology isn't perfected yet. The supply's too variable. Until we find some way of getting round that problem – and there's no guarantee we will – renewables just aren't viable. Even if they were, you couldn't use them for everything. Wind-powered cars and trains? I don't think so.

"If you changed over to renewable energy overnight the disruption, the chaos would be horrendous. You can't stop burning fossil fuels until you've made the alternatives workable."

Charlotte regarded Caroline with a mixture of pity and disdain. The girl was pretty, but she was completely taken in by the lies and false promises of the plutocrats. "Sorry, but I'm not impressed. You can make up an excuse for just about anything if you set your mind to it."

"And may I say," Caroline continued, "that in this particular case the pollution was the fault of your friends here."

"It was necessary," said MacDuggan.

Charlotte resumed her polemicising. "It's capitalism that's the problem. Capitalism that's damaging the environment."

"So, you're not just an environmentalist, you're a Marxist revolutionary as well." Nowadays, Caroline thought, there was less and less compartmentalisation between left-wing movements. The various forms of radicalism had crystallised together into a giddy, vicious hatred of the general status quo and anything to do with it.

"There's a lot of truth in what you say," she conceded. "I know it's all gone too far…monetarism, the free market, globalisation. It's causing social unrest. Wealth isn't being distributed fairly. The system needs to change."

"Big of you to admit it," said Charlotte. She sounded unconvinced of Caroline's humanitarian credentials.

"But there's still no alternative to private enterprise. Man's a natural capitalist."

Charlotte swung round to her, seeming astonished as much as angry. "Rubbish!" she shouted, her suspicions confirmed.

"It's true," said Chris. "People want to do well for themselves. And they've always been better off under a capitalist system."

"Who are you trying to kid?" Charlotte snapped. She proceeded to lecture them at some length about extremes of poverty in the world. The shattering consequences of the Third World Debt, the oppressive regimes that international oil companies like theirs supported in places like Africa and the Middle East. The wastefulness of the throwaway society. The general misery and disruption resulting from the logic of commercial expansion. It was obvious she believed every word she was saying was true.

But then, she did have a point.

"Capitalism is evil," she declared. "It debases and oppresses people. It creates racism..."

"How?" asked Caroline, familiar with the allegation but still baffled. A wide range of societies, regardless of ethnicity, practised some degree of private enterprise. And there were many businessmen who supported racial integration because it meant they would have a wider market to operate in. If anything, it was the converse of Charlotte's position which was true.

She thought of a further objection. "Surely the trouble with Marxism is that you can only achieve it at the cost of *political* totalitarianism. That's one of the lessons of the twentieth century. Look at Russia, look at China, look at Eastern Europe, look at every other Communist state. Their poor human rights record, the way they banned all freedom of expression. If Marx had lived twice as long as he did he wouldn't have been a Marxist. My friend's right; people are naturally capitalist. They want to make a profit, because it allows them to improve the quality of their lives. How could you be sure someone wasn't operating a private business somewhere without all kinds of surveillance and restrictive laws?

"Of course, there's always an excuse for it. You people always claimed that the Soviet Union and countries like that weren't typical socialist states. The typical socialist state was always a very elusive thing. I would have thought that in the 80-plus years since the Russian Revolution you'd have been able to create one. We were never justified in condemning it because it never actually existed. But if it never existed, what bloody good was it?"

She shifted slightly in her seat. Intent on the argument, Charlotte and her allies didn't appear to notice the movement. When she'd been tied up she'd tried to remember what they said about contracting your muscles so that when they relaxed you could slip out of your bonds. She wasn't sure if it had worked, but the ropes did seemed to be giving, if gradually. In any case she had to do it slowly, a bit at a time, or they'd realise.

She risked another tug of her wrist.

Chris was speaking again. "You could say Communism only started in Russia because people never had a chance to see capitalism at its best. The Tsar was a prat and he wouldn't or couldn't bring in democracy or do what was necessary to give the people wealth and prosperity. If things had been different..."

For the moment Caroline abandoned trying to free herself and joined in again. "Even if you got rid of capitalism you'd still have the problem of variability of supply. It's a *technical* difficulty, no amount of political or economic engineering will solve it. For the time being we still need the oil, like it or not.

"Even in a simpler, a mediaeval, society – one that used wind and water to power industry and produce food – people were capitalists. You had your merchants and your moneylenders. To get your non-capitalist state you'd have to go right back to the Stone Age, reverse thousands of years of progress. People wouldn't allow that."

She searched for yet more arguments she might use. "Everybody's got the same *value* as human beings. But if equality means having the same level of wealth as everybody else, well then you'll never achieve it. Some people just happen to have skills that are more marketable than others'. So they're more *successful*."

Chris chipped in. "It's *individuality*. That's what causes the inequality. Maybe there's a world where we can have one without the other. But it's not this one and it never will be. And if you have to choose between the two I know which one I'd go for. I wouldn't make the mistake the Soviets did."

Charlotte's lips twisted. "It's all right for you," she snarled. "You don't have to make sacrifices. You're in a high profile job earning lots of money and you can jet about all over the world, having fun while people in Africa are *starving...*"

"If you give me greater opportunities than someone else, of course I'm going to take them," Caroline said unashamedly. "It's what the poor would do themselves, if they had the chance. I take them because..." She paused to think. "Well, I can tell you one reason. My parents wanted me to succeed, to do well in life, and I'd like to think they felt I'd met their expectations.

"Better that some people have luxuries, and comforts, and privileges than nobody does. That's sensible, surely? And fair. The world being what it is – imperfect – it's often the most you can expect. The trouble is, Charlotte, your sort want perfection. And when of course you can't achieve it, you get nasty.

"I do what I can to help those who are less fortunate than me. I stick up for people I think are being bullied at work or have been unfairly dismissed. I do my best to oppose hire-and-fire recruitment policies. I try to make sure the wealth from our refineries, wherever they are, filters down to the local population. You can't ask any more of me than I'm giving, Charlotte."

"That's right," said Chris.

"Let's suppose everyone did decide they wanted Communism. How can you be sure their views wouldn't change? I'll say it again, you couldn't have Communism *and* democracy. In a democracy, with free elections, how could you be sure people wouldn't vote you out and bring back capitalism? They might be crazy to do that, by your reckoning, but it'd be their right. And that would mean everything you'd done would have to be dismantled. You couldn't stand that, could you? It'd be a pretty big job, bearing in mind the kind of changes you'd have made. And if you ever got back in, you'd have the bother of putting it all back again."

She looked round at the aliens, unsure how much of her words they understood but sensing they were concerned, even perplexed, by them. "It's killed more people than it's really benefited. Just as you will if you get your way.

"People have ownership of the means of production – but since, in the nature of things, you'll always get an elite, since any government, and there would have to be government for the sake of order, is inevitably one even if all its members come from the same social class as most of the people, it would never be true Communism. Politicians are a clique with their own culture and group mentality. You can't say that in a planned economy communal ownership will prevent a small body of organisers from dictating what people could buy and sell, because it wouldn't be communal ownership. The nationalised industries in post-war Britain really belonged to the government, not the people."

Charlotte gave her a look of contempt. "I'm sick of listening to you trying to justify yourself."

"I'm not sure you *are* listening."

The aliens still seemed uncertain. In the end, she got the impression they were won over more by Charlotte's passion and conviction than by what she was actually saying. They could sense the difference between her and the other humans, and knew she was on their side. That was all that mattered.

"No, it must be done," said MacDuggan impatiently. Again he stepped towards Caroline with the crystal held out in front of him.

It took everyone completely by surprise when her arms whipped out from behind the back of the chair and she sprang to her feet, her ropes falling away. Before any of the aliens could react she had snatched the crystal from MacDuggan's outstretched hand.

She leaped back against the wall, the crystal held high above her head. "Get back!" she shouted. "Get back or I'll smash it!"

The aliens were still fazed by the unexpected turn of events. It was doubtful they even heard her.

She thought of the guard outside the door. "If you call to your friend out there I'll break this thing. I swear itl." She remembered the Armalite rifle, now lying on MacDuggan's desk. "And don't make a grab for the gun, either."

The reality of the situation began to sink in. Charlotte regarded Caroline with an expression of pure hatred.

MacDuggan stepped away from her, knowing what would happen if the crystal were destroyed. The electrical impulses out of which the minds inside it, like those of humans, were composed would escape into the atmosphere and be lost forever. It would be the same as if a human brain were physically destroyed. The link between thought and matter would be severed, the mind would no cease to inhabit the body and you would no longer have what was regarded as a living being. You would die, whatever death ultimately entailed. Whether the impulses would simply be released into the ether to travel through it for evermore, or be transferred somewhere where they could be given a new body to occupy, as human religions insisted was possible, was something the aliens' science had never been able to establish.

Caroline was breathing a sigh of relief. She hadn’t been quite sure what the stuff was exactly, but it must be delicate enough to shatter fairly easily going by MacDuggan’s reaction.

A strange noise rose in the foreman's throat. His eyes were burning with something that looked like hatred and yet had an unfamiliar quality to it which made it disturbing. A thick stream of saliva welled from his mouth.

"So all of you stay right where you are," Caroline ordered. "In fact better still, I want you all to move as far away from me as possible, right to the other side of the room. Oh – before you do, you can untie my friend Chris over there."

They hastened to obey. Once free, Chris took the Armalite from the desk and moved to her side. "Now let's talk about this like reasonable people," she suggested.

Her eyes never left them for a second.

Nine

The executive who rang Chief Superintendent Lewars within a few minutes of the latter having arrived at the station and seated himself at his desk sounded worried. "Piper One didn't make their usual call this morning. So we radioed them and couldn't get any reply." He didn't need to say anything more. After everything else that had happened on the rig, there could only be a sinister reason for this new development.

"Did you call the MOD?"

"Yes, and they said they were happy for you to deal with the matter if you wanted to." In view of their responsibility for the oil rig it had been thought prudent to train Lewars and his team in anti-terrorist procedures. Normally dealing with terrorist incidents on offshore structures was the job of the SAS, but these days they were frequently overstretched, and generally, what with the increasing threat from both terrorism and domestic crime the police had of late been moving more and more towards a semi-military role.

"I don't see any reason why we shouldn't. OK, we'll have a response team out there as quick as possible. Give me a call if there's any news."

He dialled the Chief Constable's number. Within minutes he had received the necessary authorisation. He selected the officers he wanted for the job, and had the armourer break out the guns. Less than an hour after Aberdeen had sounded the alarm, they were in the air and passing over the coast in the direction of Piper One.

Caroline had seated herself at MacDuggan's desk, Chris standing beside her, while the aliens and Charlotte had retreated to the other end of the room, as requested.

"When the police get here, I'll try and explain everything," said Caroline. "Then we'll all go back to the mainland and you can talk with our scientists and politicians." The aliens just stared fixedly at her, their emotions unintelligible.

"And what about me?" Charlotte said drily. "I suppose I'm going to be thrown straight into prison, am I?"

"That'll be for a judge to decide."

Silence fell. From time to time, Caroline and Charlotte traded uneasy looks. Caroline toyed with the crystal to cover her nerves.

Otherwise, nothing much happened. Until, for the second time in the last three hours, the fire alarm went off.

Caroline stiffened. Charlotte grinned nastily at the consternation in her face. "What are you going to do now, Caroline?" she said mockingly. "Don't tell me we're all going to stay here till we burn to death."

Chris had to admit it would be preferable if they didn't.

Thinking fast, Caroline turned to MacDuggan. "Open the door and call out to the guard. Tell him to put his gun down on the floor, well away from the door, and come in. That's what I want to hear you say, nothing else. Chris, you get ready to jump him if he tries anything."

Outside Sean was standing with a frown-like expression on his face, uncertain what to do. The lack of any urgent response to the alarm from within the office puzzled and disconcerted him.

He glanced about in case he might spot the source of the fire. He saw a cloud of smoke hanging in the air at the end of the corridor and wondered if he should go to investigate. Then the office door opened and he heard MacDuggan's voice.

As instructed, he laid the rifle on the floor and went inside. His face twitched several times as he took in the situation, but he showed no other reaction.

"Now," said Caroline. "We're all going up on deck to wait for the relief helicopter. While we're waiting we can carry on the conversation until we reach some kind of understanding. Don't anyone make a move for that gun; you know what I'll do with your thingummybob." She held up the crystal.

MacDuggan made a move towards the door. "Ladies first, if you don't mind," she said, and motioned him back.

Chris opened the door and he and Caroline backed out of the room, Charlotte and the aliens following. Chris turned to pick up the gun from where Sean had laid it, and found himself facing Jamie Grant and about a dozen oilmen.

Grant was clearly delighted at finding Chris and Caroline still alive. "It's all right," he grinned. "We're on your side. We decided it was time to fight back." He spoke to a couple of his companions. "Doug, Shughie, go and put it out. Just smother it with a bit of canvas, that should do the trick." The two oilmen went off, returning a couple of minutes later.

Grant explained how they had attempted to draw Sean away from the door, with the aim of ambushing him and taking his gun, by starting a fire and setting off the alarm. "There's plenty of oil around, so we just emptied some on the floor of one of the store-rooms and struck a match. Just enough to trigger the alarm without doing any real damage." They had hidden in another room, from which one of them had peeped out cautiously and seen Sean put down the gun before going into the office, whereupon they'd made to take the weapon.

"What's been happening with *you*?" Grant asked.

Grinning broadly, Caroline described how she'd managed to turn the tables on her captors. Grant clapped her on the shoulder. "You may be a Sassenach, but you're quite a lass." He became serious. "Now what's this all about? What the hell do they *want*?" His whole world had turned upside down. He looked to MacDuggan, remembering the man was supposed to be his superior. "Chief, what's going on?" He frowned at the superintendent's strange, blank expression.

"It's going to take some explaining," Chris told him. He proceeded to tell the whole story, or attempt to.

When the two aliens who had been sent to find and kill the surviving unpossessed oilmen came round a corner into the corridor, they didn't at first see what was going on. The cluster of people hid

MacDuggan and the other possessed humans from their view, and they didn't notice that Caroline had the crystal. They just saw their enemies gathered together and seized the opportunity.

Immediately they started blazing away. Chris and Caroline heard the chatter of rifle fire, saw bodies drop to the floor around them. The oilmen instinctively ran, and in a moment the corridor was a confused jumble of people rushing to escape. One of the possessed men staggered and fell dying, shot by his own side. Sam Meredith had picked up Sean's rifle and was waiting for a clear shot at the two aliens. Someone barged into him and it went flying from his hand. A succession of running feet trampled over it.

Chris realised what had happened, and his brain leaped into action. He had the rifle, but it was two against one. Suicide. And the mass of running bodies was blocking his view.

He looked round for Caroline and saw MacDuggan rush at her, snatching the crystal from her hand. The foreman tried to grab her and for a moment the two of them struggled fiercely.

They were too close together for Chris to fire without hitting Caroline. He thrust the rifle into Bob's hand as the oilman ran past him. Then he shoulder-charged MacDuggan, his burly rugby-player's frame crashing into the foreman and sending him flying. He shouted at Caroline to run.

MacDuggan scrambled to his feet, picking up the crystal which he had dropped when Chris tackled him. The thought of trying to get it back off him crossed Barrett's mind but he might be hit, deliberately or accidentally, while they struggled. He hurried after Caroline.

In his haste to put as much space between himself and the two gunmen as possible, he didn't realise they'd stopped firing. By now they had registered Caroline's presence; and as far as they knew, being unaware of what had happened in the office, she was still vital to the plan. They must not risk harming her.

Regaining his bearings, and seeing the reason for their hesitation, MacDuggan shouted to the gunmen. "Kill them! All of them!"

Bob decided to stand and fight with the rifle. He shot one of the aliens but the other blasted him down immediately, snatching up the rifle from beside his body. It had been a bad mistake and he paid for it with his life.

Two more aliens fell dead, but the other humans had disappeared from sight. "After them!" screamed MacDuggan. He, Charlotte and the remaining aliens, one of whom had picked up the fourth rifle, ran off in search of their quarry.

Several corridors and twenty minutes later, Caroline and her companions staggered to a halt, panting. They seemed to have eluded the enemy for the moment. Listening carefully, they heard no sounds of pursuit.

"We forgot about those two," said Chris, in a tone of bitter self-reproach.

Caroline nodded curtly, equally upset by their mistake but not wanting to admit it. "And we don't have the crystal any more."

"The main thing is they haven't got us," said Chris. "Now we've got to stay free until the police come. Trouble is, we've no idea when that'll be."

"If we stay in one place they're bound to find us sooner or later," said Jamie Grant. "Best thing to do is to keep running around as long as possible."

"We might just tire ourselves out," pointed out Caroline. She felt pretty well knackered already.

"And we can't go on starting fires," Jamie sighed.

"What's it all about anyway?" asked Don Connell. "My head's reeling with it all." Chris hadn't quite finished explaining everything when the gunfight had broken out.

"Let's just say MacDuggan and your other colleagues have been, well, taken over. They're up to the same sort of thing as the terrorists."

"Are you saying they've been...hypnotised?"

"Sort of. Look, is there anywhere we could go where they wouldn't dare shoot at us? Somewhere with vital equipment?"

"Nearest place is the generator room. Produces most of the lighting and heating for the rig. Lot of things there that could cause a pretty nasty explosion if they caught fire."

"Let's go then," Caroline said.

Several more corridors and a flight of stairs took them to their destination. "If we sabotaged any of this equipment..." began Caroline, studying the rows of consoles and the two huge generators which took up the centre of the massive room.

Jamie shook his head. "Only as a last resort. It'd work to our disadvantage as much as theirs. We'd soon be freezing to death, as well as stumbling about in the dark trying to find our noses."

"Is there any way they could flush us out of here?" she asked. It'd be as well to make sure.

Jamie thought carefully. They saw a worried look come over his face. "Well...they *could* put something in the ventilation system, I suppose. As a matter of fact, I was thinking earlier on..." His eyes gleamed. "We may as well do it now. If we get hold of some gas cylinders and pump the stuff into the system, it'd knock them out. Or worse."

"But we'd be putting ourselves at risk too, wouldn't we?"

"We stand a chance if we cover our mouths and noses, and go up on deck once we think the gas has had time to take effect."

"Where's it kept?"

"In the chemical store."

"Then let's get over there right away," said Caroline, rising.

"We'd better not all go," said Jamie. "If we get captured we've had it. But if some of us stay here then we may have a chance." He looked sadly round the little gathering. There weren't that many of them left as it was.

"Well, *I'm* going," declared Caroline. She supposed she ought to, as it had been her suggestion. Besides, it wasn't her way to be sitting around while there was work to be done.

"It's all right, hen," said Grant gently. "You've been in enough danger already. Let a couple of us do it."

His concern wasn't meant to be sexist, but nonetheless Caroline was unimpressed. Without a word she headed for the door.

"I'll go with you," offered an oilman called Robson.

"You'll need about four or five cylinders," shouted out Grant. "You can pump the stuff in from in the store."

"Take care, Caz," Chris urged as she and Robson set off.

"Of course I will," she said reproachfully.

Along with the rest of them, Chris settled down to wait. He suddenly thought of the explosives and supposed he'd better tell the oilmen about them, although he doubted they were in any immediate danger. It would rather spoil Charlotte's plans if she blew herself, her allies and the crystal into little pieces.

"You didn't find any by any chance, did you?" he asked Jamie.

"Aye. In the cinema and in the drill room. We chucked them in the sea."

"There'll be plenty more about the rig," said Chris. "But we'll worry about that later."

His gaze fell on a man of about sixty with a greying black beard and a lined, wise face, who sat slumped against the far wall. This was Angus Kincaid, the rig's doctor. His manner had been genial and humorous when Chris had talked with him yesterday, but now he looked sad and withdrawn. A man accustomed to preserving lives does not like to see people dying in scores all around him. That his assistant had been one of those massacred on the deck by Charlotte had particularly upset him. He'd also found all the running about he'd had to do extremely stressful, being the oldest member of the crew.

Chris went to squat beside him. "You all right, Doc?"

Kincaid looked up with a weary smile. "Don't worry, laddie, I'm fine. A doctor always knows when he isn't. The actual running wasn't too bad, it was the way I felt afterwards. But I'm all right."

"I wanted to ask your opinion on something," Chris whispered. "A doctor's a sort of scientist, I suppose. And scientists have to keep an open mind."

"Spit it out," said Kincaid.

He told the doctor everything he and Caroline had learned while prisoners in MacDuggan's office. "Do you...do you believe me?" he asked afterwards.

Kincaid was staring at him in astonishment. Then a wry smile came over the doctor's face. "Well, I knew the explanation for all this had to be *something* weird."

"When we were in the office with them, I had the impression once or twice that they were...unwell. I think the alien thought patterns are having a damaging effect on them. It's worse the longer they're being controlled. But they can't let go until they've managed to take over the relief helicopter and get safely away from here." He scratched his chin. "If we ever get the chance, how the hell are we going to cure them? I was thinking the crystal might do it, but I've no idea how it works."

Kincaid's brow furrowed. "I don't know. It's all way outside anyone's previous experience."

"I was thinking maybe the gas..."

"Maybe." A thought occurred to Kincaid. "The aliens on this rig can't be the only ones, surely? Why don't they call their friends and get them to help out?"

"Because they don't want to show their hand. They want to reconquer the planet by stealth." And if they won the struggle for control of Piper One, they might well succeed.

"Nearly there," said Robson.

Caroline sighed in relief. Time might not be on their side; it wouldn't be long, she guessed, before the aliens had the idea of using the gas on them, assuming they hadn't already.

She supposed that since the bodies they inhabited were human there was no reason why the gas shouldn't have the desired effect on them.

"Here we are." Robson swung open the door and they hurried through into a vault-like room with ribbed metal walls. The shiny black metal canisters, torpedo-like in shape, were stacked in rows a few feet away.

"What's this stuff used for?" asked Caroline, hefting one of the cylinders.

"Welding. And making the compound we use to seal fractures in the support columns."

There was a ventilation grille high up in one wall. As it was just beyond their reach, they heaved a crate over to a point directly beneath it.

"We'd better cover ourselves up before we do anything else," Robson told her. They each wrapped handkerchiefs tightly over their mouths and nostrils.

It would be a fairly simple matter to stand five cylinders on top of the crate, pay out the hose from each one and insert it through the holes in the grille, then twist the valves to send the gas hissing into the ventilation system.

Caroline went to select a cylinder from the nearest stack. Her back to Robson, she didn't see his eyes suddenly glaze over, all human expression vanishing from his face. But a few moments later she felt the spanner he had armed himself with crash down on the back of her head, though only briefly before black oblivion swallowed up her brain.

Ten

Charlotte and her companions moved slowly and cautiously along the corridor, constantly on the alert for danger. There was a savage determination on MacDuggan's face which Charlotte found made her uneasy.

She heard the footsteps before the aliens did, as if their reflexes were duller. "Someone's coming!" she hissed. The five of them paused, and waited.

Robson appeared around the corner, Caroline slung over his shoulder. MacDuggan smiled wolfishly. Charlotte was puzzled for a moment, then noticed the look in Robson's eyes and understood.

"Brilliant," she grinned. "That's just what we need. Let's get back to the office."

Once there Robson dumped Caroline into a chair. She was just starting to recover consciousness. They turned to look at her.

"She must die," said MacDuggan. "She is the symbol of all we are fighting against. She must be punished."

"Eventually, yes," said Charlotte after a moment. "But not yet. Remember we need hostages. And right now we have to persuade her friends to come out from wherever they're hiding." She regarded Caroline significantly.

"Barrett will not give in. The others will not allow him to."

Charlotte was looking deeply thoughtful. "Perhaps that depends on exactly *how* she's going to die."

*

Slowly, painfully, consciousness returned to Caroline. The first thing she was aware of was a dull throbbing pain in her head.

She shifted, groaning, and immediately encountered some form of resistance.

She couldn't move.

She was lying on a ridged, discontinuous metal surface, her arms and legs spread out and fastened down at the wrists and ankles with rope.

She looked up, and all thought of her headache evaporated instantly as she saw where she was.

Some fifty feet above her stomach, stationary for the moment, was the gleaming snout of the drill. She realised she must be tied directly over the opening in the floor.

She heard feet ringing on the metal and craned her neck painfully to see Charlotte and MacDuggan coming towards her. They stopped and looked down at their prisoner.

"Comfortable, Caroline?" inquired Charlotte.

"You...you're not going to..."

"Oh, *I* wouldn't. He might, though." She nodded towards MacDuggan. In the foreman's face Caroline now saw a more human, but nonetheless alarming, kind of savagery. "I'd watch him if I were you."

She dropped to her haunches beside Caroline's spreadeagled body. The thing is, you're useful to us right now. When he finds out what we've got lined up for you your boyfriend'll have no choice but to come quietly."

"He's not actually my boyfriend."

"No, but he does care about you. That was the impression I got, anyway. I can't think why. Personally I think you're snobbish, opinionated, conceited and arrogant."

The words of an old pop song came to Caroline's mind. "Don't ask me what I think of you, I might not give the answer that you want me to."

"I don't care what you think of me," said Charlotte.

"So, you're going to drill a great big hole in me if they don't surrender?"

"What a clever little girl you are."

"Even if Chris does what you want, how can you be sure the others will?"

"Too bad if they don't."

A strangled whimpering noise from beside her made Charlotte start. She turned to MacDuggan and saw saliva trickle once again from the corner of his mouth.

"Are you all right?" she asked, trying to hide her increasing concern.

"Yes...there is no problem," he breathed. "There's no...no...problem..."

"He doesn't look too well if you ask me," said Caroline.

Brushing the matter aside, Charlotte turned back to her. "You're keeping your cool, aren't you? Good. I like that."

"Are you telling the truth? You won't kill me if Chris and the others give themselves up?"

Disturbingly, Charlotte didn't immediately reply. "It's like this," she said finally. "To them you're a symbol of all the harm the oil giants have done to this planet. You've got to go." She glanced up at the drill. "You must admit, it'd be appropriate. That someone who makes their career out of an industry which kills millions of living things should themselves die by it."

"And do you care?"

"Not particularly." Then Charlotte's manner changed, became almost apologetic. "Look, sweetie, it's quite simple. They want you dead, and they're determined to get their way. It's out of my hands, there's nothing I can do."

She turned away, her face a slab of solid stone.

"They're mad, you know that?" Caroline shouted desperately.

"That's why it's all the more important I humour them," Charlotte replied.

Chris Barrett gazed round at his companions apprehensively. It had already occurred to them that any of their number might have been possessed by the aliens, but there was absolutely nothing that could be done about the problem. They had to put the worrying thought to the back of their minds and try to trust one another.

That wasn't the only thing troubling him at the moment. "They should have got that gas fixed up by now," he said anxiously.

"Aye," nodded Jamie. He raised his voice. "Cover your faces, lads."

"I mean I think something's happened to them."

They heard the crackle of the PA system, then MacDuggan's voice. "Barrett! Can you hear me?"

Chris closed his eyes. "That means it has." He cursed himself for letting Caroline go off with Robson.

"Barrett, there's something you must...must know...we've got your friend. If you want to see her alive again you must...must surrender now." Apart from the hesitations, MacDuggan's voice sounded almost normal. But the tones of hatred and malice were unmistakeable. "She's tied underneath the drill, Barrett. You know what that thing can do to a human body?"

One of the oilmen gasped in horror. "He's got to be joking. He wouldn't..."

"There are people on this planet who would," said Chris darkly. "Caroline and I have met some of them. I suppose it depends how much she's annoyed somebody," he added reflectively.

"But a girl like that..."

"And don't forget, they're not...human. Not at the moment. They don't think the way we do, see us as we do ourselves."

"Come to the drill chamber. If you aren't there within twenty minutes, you'll hear the sound of it starting up. That sound will mean death to her. You haven't got long to make your mind up, so I'd better sign...sign *off*...now...nowwwww......" The alien note had crept back into his voice. A gurgling, sucking noise issued from the tannoy, then it clicked off.

There followed a long, shocked moment of silence. "We cannae let her die like that," murmured one of the oilmen.

"Let's just think a moment," said Chris. He considered the situation carefully for a minute or so, then turned to Jamie. "If MacDuggan's really prepared to do it, there'd have to be someone in the drill control room operating the thing, wouldn't there?"

"Aye. You'd need to override the computer."

"But the rest of them must all be in the drill chamber, I imagine. Look, I've got an idea. But we're going to have to move fast if we're to save Caroline's life. Come on."

"Where to?" asked Jamie.

"The chemical store." He explained his plan to them on the way there.

They stopped to fetch some oxyacetylene torches from the equipment room next door, with Jamie, Connell and Doug taking as many of them as each could carry. Another oilman took a couple of the gas cylinders from the chemical store. Then they headed for the drill chamber. On the way they saw no sign of any of their enemies; it seemed Chris' supposition was correct.

In the corridor that led to the drill chamber, about twenty feet from the door, they stood the cylinders up against the wall, each with a torch placed in front of it and switched on full. Then they hurried on, while behind them the metal of the cylinders began to blister under the yellow flames.

"Once we are away from here," MacDuggan was saying to Charlotte, "control can be withdrawn. For a time. But you will need to secure us."

Charlotte nodded. "I'll see to it."

Chris won't let me die like this, Caroline was thinking. He'll be along soon. But there was still the worry of what would happen after that.

She'd been in danger of her life before, on more occasions than she cared to recall. But there was always the fear that the next time might be the last time, the time when your luck ran out.

Once more she glanced uneasily up at the drill.

There was still no sign of Chris and the others.

Charlotte came into view. "Time's up, Caroline. Sorry, but we have to show we mean business." She jerked her head at MacDuggan. "Do it."

MacDuggan got out Charlotte's radio. "Start the drill."

Caroline caught her breath, a spasm of inexpressible horror shooting through her.

In the control room above the chamber, Robson's finger stabbed at a button on the main computer console.

"You can't do this!" Caroline shouted. "It...it's not..." She remembered that inhuman was precisely what they were, at that moment.

She heard a dull booming like the roar of some huge and hungry beast. Then the steel tube of the drill began to move.

She stared up at it fixedly, as if paralysed by the thought of her fate. Solid tungsten carbide, weighing fifty tons and rotating at 160 rpm, powered by an 8,000-watt generator. It would churn through human tissue, shredding flesh, nerves, muscle and organs like wet paper. It was descending at a rate of about ten feet a minute.

Then those in the chamber heard the sound of running feet from the corridor, and turned expectantly towards the door.

"Chris!" Caroline yelled. "They're going to kill me anyway!"

The noise of the drill drowned out her words as it slid remorselessly downward.

Charlotte jumped on her, took a roll of adhesive tape from her pocket, ripped off a length and slapped it over Caroline's lips.

A moment later Chris burst in, Jamie and the others right behind him. He took in the scene in horror.

"Switch it off!" he shouted.

Charlotte glanced at MacDuggan. He hesitated, then gave the order. The drill ceased turning, and came to a shuddering stop.

"Great, we're all here," said Charlotte. "Glad you could make it, Mr Barrett. We were beginning to worry about you. Now stand over there with the others." Chris noted how Charlotte seemed to have taken command, and the listless robot-like manner of the possessed humans.

"Go up on deck and keep a look-out for that helicopter," Charlotte ordered Kenny. "The moment you spot it let us know." He made for the door.

"Untie her," snapped Chris, indicating Caroline.

A nasty grin appeared on MacDuggan's face. "I don't think you're in any position to give orders, Mr Barrett."

Kenny had almost reached the door when the deafening roar of an explosion filled the chamber and it was ripped from its hinges, travelling a few yards through the air before crashing down with an echoing clang. Blown violently off his feet by the force of the blast, he landed heavily on his back, quite senseless.

Immediately the rig's disaster control system cut in, sealing off the corridor and pumping in fire-retardant foam.

Chris and his friends were shaken by the blast, but at least they were expecting it. For a few seconds their enemies' attention was distracted.

It had been a desperate gamble but the only chance they had. They threw themselves at the possessed oilmen.

Charlotte's wits were just quick enough for her to avoid being jumped. She shot the oilman who was lunging towards her, then turned to where Chris was struggling to wrest Sean's rifle from him. The two of them staggered in all directions, their strength roughly equal. Charlotte hesitated, waiting for the chance of a clear shot at Barrett.

Dave shot one of the oilmen but another dived for his legs, bringing him down. He lost his grip on the rifle and it skidded a little way across the floor. Two oilmen, one possessed and one normal, were soon locked in a bitter struggle for it. A third snatched it up only for Charlotte, still unable to get a clear shot at Chris, to turn her attention to him and blast him down. Before she could select a new target, Jamie Grant's big hands had smashed down on the back of her neck. She crumpled and fell unconscious, the gun clattering on the floor. Jamie and Dave then began fighting for it.

Sean was still grappling with Chris. Shughie had taken Kenny's rifle, but was faced with the same problem as Charlotte; he couldn't shoot at his enemies because his friends were in the way. Nearby, a group of oilmen were locked in savage hand-to-hand combat.

MacDuggan stood watching the scene, his face twisted with rage and hatred. He snatched out the radio and shouted an order to Robson. "Start the drill – and this time it stays on!"

The machine whirred into life, resuming its descent towards the helpless girl tied beneath it.

MacDuggan hovered at the edge of the fight, not wanting to miss Caroline's spectacular end.

One of the unpossessed oilmen, McBarnett, ran for the stairs to the control room and scrambled up them.

Chris had seen and heard the drill start up. Abandoning the fight with Sean, he ran to Caroline and flung himself down beside her.

Sean decided it was more important to deal with the oilmen, and immediately threw himself on one of them.

Moving with frantic speed, his heart feeling as if it were about to explode, Chris struggled to undo Caroline's bonds.

He wasn't going to make it in time. "Help me!" he screamed, almost hysterical.

Then with a yell MacDuggan hurled himself on the young executive. Briefly before the impact of the massive body smashed him to the ground Chris saw his expression – a terrifying portrait of insane rage and malice, with several different hatreds reflected in that twisted face, each vying for supremacy in his mind. A stream of garbled words poured from his mouth, some of them strange and alien, others English but unnaturally harsh and guttural. The eyes gleamed with inhuman, unearthly evil, and the foreman's chin glistened with a thick coating of saliva.

McBarnett burst into the control room, saw Robson standing at the console, and ran straight at him.

Caroline shut her eyes. In another few moments, it would be too late to save her. Even if the drill's descent were halted its momentum would carry it on for a few more seconds until it cut her in two. Her self-control finally broke and she screamed out through the gag.

In the control room McBarnett and Robson rolled over and over on the floor, their arms around each other. Suddenly McBarnett broke free, leaped to his feet and dashed to the console. His fist slammed down on the off button, and the drill juddered to a halt.

He pressed a second button and it began to rise up into the ceiling.

Make your mind up, thought Caroline hysterically.

Recovering consciousness, Kenny had snatched the rifle from Rory and before he could react shot him point blank in the chest. Meanwhile Shughie and another oilman had overpowered Sean and grabbed his weapon. Putting all his considerable strength behind the blow, Shughie smashed the butt of the gun across the back of the terrorist's head. He crumpled and fell.

In the struggle for possession of Charlotte's rifle the alien had got the upper hand. He wrenched the gun from his opponent's grasp and shot him down.

Shughie dropped, brought down by a bullet in the shoulder from Kenny.

Robson glanced around for a weapon to use against McBarnett, saw a crowbar lying on the floor near the wall and ran for it.

McBarnett rushed to intercept him but was just too late. Robson snatched it up, whirled round and lunged at him, raising the crowbar high above his head.

MacDuggan had thrown himself on top of Chris, clamped his big hands round the Englishman's throat and was squeezing hard, trying to crush the windpipe. The colour drained from Chris' face and his eyes bulged. Summoning up all the aggression, hatred even, that a sportsman needs to win he drew up his legs and kicked MacDuggan in the chest as hard as he could. The foreman's grip was broken and he flipped over backwards, hitting the floor with a thud.

As Robson lashed out with the crowbar McBarnett dodged the blow, grabbed the tool and tried to wrench it from the alien's hand. Robson let go of it, allowing McBarnett to take it, and threw a punch at his head instead. It was a bad move because McBarnett dodged, Robson's fist travelling through empty air, and then smashed him on the head with the crowbar. The blow should have knocked him out instantly, but instead he fell to his knees with both hands grasping his skull. Then he keeled over and lay still, apparently unconscious.

McBarnett hesitated. He wanted to go down and join the fight but he was troubled by the thought of Robson coming round and restarting the drill. His eyes hurriedly searched the control room for something to tie him up with, but there was nothing immediately to hand.

To disable the drill he only needed to pull out the right wires. He ran to the control panel and began prising open an inspection hatch with the crowbar.

Behind him Robson was getting slowly to his feet. He crept stealthily up on McBarnett. Intent on what he was doing, McBarnett didn't hear him approach until it was too late.

The hatch came free and he moved it to one side. Putting down the crowbar, he reached inside the opening, but just as his fingers were about to close round the tangle of wiring Robson grabbed him and pulled him away from the console. Before he could react, the crowbar took him hard across the forehead and sent him into oblivion.

An instant after Chris' kick had floored him, MacDuggan had risen to his feet with a bellow of animal rage. His strength was terrifying.

The strength of a man possessed – and of course he was. He cannoned into Chris and the two of them reeled about crazily, locked in a savage embrace.

Above the struggling pair, the drill was coming down again. Caroline's head slumped back in despair.

Chris struggled ferociously to break MacDuggan's grip, but without success. The drill was now thirty feet above Caroline.

Twenty-five feet.

Twenty.

Meanwhile Angus Kincaid had been keeping apart from the battle. He was too old to participate in it and nobody expected him to. Which perhaps gave him an advantage.

He had been working his way towards where Caroline lay. Now, while Chris and MacDuggan grappled, he threw himself down and struggled to untie her. He managed to release one ankle. Then MacDuggan threw Chris off, saw what Kincaid was doing and lunged savagely at him.

Fifteen feet.

For a brief moment Kincaid managed to hold MacDuggan. As the foreman thrust him away, sending him sprawling on the floor, Chris hurled himself once more on the supervisor's back. He wrapped his arms around MacDuggan's neck and pulled his head sharply back. Don Connell joined him and between the two of them they managed to wrest MacDuggan to the floor and pin him down.

Ten feet.

Dazed and winded from MacDuggan's attack, Kincaid shook his head to clear it. While Chris and Connell held down the furiously struggling supervisor, he hurried to finish untying Caroline. Her other foot came free.

Then one hand. He had almost succeeded in releasing the other when MacDuggan broke free from Chris and Connell, sprang to his feet and rushed at Kincaid, knocking the doctor aside. Kincaid fell stunned.

Caroline tugged frantically at the remaining cords around her wrist. She felt them loosen and fall away.

Then MacDuggan was on his knees beside her, his massive hand clamping down on hers and pinning it to the floor. She tried to twist free of him but his grip shifted barely a fraction. He would hold her long enough for the drill to do its work.

Chris and Connell tried to pull MacDuggan away from Caroline. To resist he had to stand, letting go of her, at the same time twisting in a bid to throw them off. He lost his balance, taking Chris with him as he fell sprawling.

Connell made to help, only to jerk and fall to his knees as a stray bullet from the nearby gunfight tore through his right arm just above the elbow. He fought to rise, gritting his teeth against the pain.

Once again, MacDuggan broke away and bounded to his feet, Chris rising with him. The wounded Connell staggered towards them, arms reaching out in an ineffectual attempt to grasp MacDuggan. The foreman smashed him viciously aside, and spun to face Chris. The two gripped each other in a savage embrace and lurched about blindly, each trying to bring the other down. By now they were both starting to tire.

The spinning cutters were now almost level with their heads, and MacDuggan was thrusting Chris towards them.

A final burst of strength would finish him off. MacDuggan rallied all his energies. As did Chris, frantic to avoid those whirling razor-sharp teeth.

Five feet.

One final tug, and Caroline's wrist slipped from its restraints. She scrambled out of the path of the drill.

Then MacDuggan stumbled and fell, again bringing Chris down with him. Heaving himself from underneath Barrett, he rolled clear of him – and into the mouth of the drill shaft.

Connell, raising himself into a kneeling position, saw MacDuggan's legs and the lower part of his body disappear from view. The foreman clutched frantically at the smooth edges of the opening, desperate to check his fall. He managed to gain a purchase, hanging on for his life above the three hundred foot drop to the sea bed.

He stared into the rapidly rotating cutters of the drill, just a foot or two above him.

There wasn't enough clearance for him to pull himself up over the edge.

The drill came nearer, nearer.

He couldn't let go, he couldn't...

The image of the whirling cutters, barely an inch away, filled his vision and burnt itself into his brain.

They seemed to brush his forehead.

The hideous scream which tore itself from MacDuggan's lips was human, unmistakeably and appallingly human. It could be heard well above the rumble of the drill. The foreman's hands vanished from sight and the sound of the monstrous machine swallowed up the scream.

Below, it echoed in the hollowness of the drill shaft as he plummeted down it.

Robson had witnessed these events from the control room through the huge window that overlooked the drill chamber. He ran for the ladder and pelted down it, anxious to join the fight.

Chris ripped the gag from Caroline's mouth. Overcome for the moment by the shock and stress of her ordeal she curled up into a ball, her face buried in her knees, shaking uncontrollably.

Chris looked round to see how the battle was progressing. A number of oilmen lay dead or injured on the floor. A gunfight was taking place between Kenny, Robson and three other possessed humans on one side, and two normal oilmen on the other. Jamie Grant was locked in a fist fight with a sixth alien. He couldn't be sure as the situation was a little confused but it looked like everyone else was out of the running. Connell had slipped into semi-consciousness and was lying on his side moaning softly, blood continuing to seep from his injured arm.

There was no time to be gentle. Chris hauled Caroline roughly to her feet and shook her until she had regained her wits. "We've got to get out of here," he shouted. Grabbing her by the hand, he dashed for the stairs to the drill control room. Indignantly she broke free, then took in the situation and ran after him.

They burst into the control room to be greeted by McBarnett, now more or less back to full consciousness. Hearing feet pounding on the stairs, they looked round to see Jamie Grant, several other oilmen and Dr Kincaid.

"We can't go on running," Grant shouted. "We've got to stand and fight."

"We will," said Chris savagely. He thought fast.

"The main generator room," he yelled.

It was the only chance that he could see.

Charlotte was struggling into a sitting position, scowling from the pain in her head and neck. Her vision cleared and she saw Chris, Caroline and the others scramble up the ladder, the surviving possessed oilmen in pursuit. She would have followed, but she had even more important things on her mind right now.

MacDuggan was nowhere to be seen. But she did see the crystal, lying near the edge of the drill shaft where it had fallen from the foreman's pocket at some point during his fight with Chris Barrett. Her eyes gleamed triumphantly and she snatched it up.

She noticed one of the Armalites lying on the floor not far away. She picked it up and examined it; empty.

Tossing it aside, she made towards the ladder. She halted as one of the dozen or so bodies strewn about the chamber stirred and got shakily to its feet. It was Sean. He'd been unconscious, that was all. There was no sign of any injury on him.

Physically, that was. The mad glare in his eyes, the fixed expression of psychotic hatred, the trembling of his body and the saliva drooling from his mouth in long strings all told of the damage being inflicted on his mind. Seeing her, he eyed her in a disturbing manner. She wondered whether he knew any more what side he was meant to be on.

Nearby, Dave too was struggling to stand up. He was in much the same condition as Sean.

She hesitated for a few moments, thinking, then stepped towards them. "Let go. Withdraw. I think they'll help us." Certainly, they'd always done what she told them to in the past.

At first they continued to stare at her. Then the glazed look left their eyes and each gave a little start, swaying on his feet. The trembling ceased.

Sean clapped a hand to his forehead. The manic expression was gone; rather, he now looked dazed and bewildered.

Charlotte went up to them. "Sean, Dave, are you OK?"

Sean shook his head. "Charlie? What...what happened?" He looked round the drill chamber, then at Charlotte. "I don’t get it. We were on the deck...they'd all gone apeshit, panicking...we started firing. Then..."

She wondered how she was going to explain the whole thing to them. It could wait until later, she decided. They'd already guessed that something out of the ordinary must have happened.

"This thing – " – she brandished the crystal – "takes over people's minds. There's a lot we can do with it.

"But I'll tell you the full story later. Right now we've got things to do."

Eleven

Caroline and her friends staggered into the main generator room, quite exhausted. They'd lost their pursuers, for the moment, but tired themselves out in the process.

Chris hurried over to one of the six generators, positioned in two rows of three, which supplied the rig with lighting and heating as well as providing power to the drill and all other machinery, whether for domestic or industrial purposes, on board Piper One. The vast machine was humming gently with the electricity coursing through it. He made his way round it, to the side that would not be visible from the door.

He squatted down by an inspection panel, and carefully lifted it out to expose a mass of wires and cables. His eye fell on the largest of them. "We need to get that free of its mounting. There should be some tools not far away, shouldn't there?"

McBarnett hurried off. A couple of minutes later he returned carrying a heavy metal box. "I think I heard them coming," he panted. "We'd better move fast."

"I'm no technician," Chris said apologetically. "I think one of you had better do this."

McBarnett opened the box and took out a massive screwdriver. He set to work loosening the baffle that held the cable in its mounting.

He pulled out the cable to its maximum length. The tangle of wires at its end crackled and spat sparks.

Then they waited. How long they'd be waiting for they couldn't know but eventually, if they stayed where they were, the aliens would track them down.

They crouched there perfectly still for some twenty minutes, their hearts pounding, their bodies rigid with tension. Then they heard the four aliens come slowly into the room.

Listening to the sound, they heard it change and realised the aliens had split into two groups, one of which would be bound before long to spot the people hiding behind the generator.

Chris glanced at the others. "We need a distraction."

Deciding to take the risk, Caroline peered out briefly and scanned the room. She judged that if several of them ran for the door that led into the adjoining workshop at least one might get through it without being shot.

It was worth the risk. Taking over from Chris, Caroline picked on a couple of oilmen, Neill and Sellars, and explained her plan to them.

Crouching low, the three of them scurried along behind the generator. They came to the gap between it and the next machine. Moving fast, they crossed it without being spotted. But the nearest of the two pairs of aliens must have heard something, because their footsteps changed direction and came towards them.

They darted across to the final generator. From there it wasn't far to the door; they broke cover and ran. A bullet zipped past Neill's head and ricocheted off the wall.

Let's hope they don't hit something important, thought Caroline morbidly.

They just made it through the door. Neill and Sellars ran for a stack of crates, intending to take cover behind it, but Caroline to their surprise darted to one side and slammed the door shut.

She pointed to a solitary crate. "Shove that against the door," she whispered fiercely. "Quickly!"

They grabbed the crate and upended it. The aliens heard the sound of the oilmen ramming it against the door, and when they flung it open found the heavy metal container barring their way. Laying down their rifles, they shoved it to one side, retrieved the guns and ran on into the workshop.

They had assumed their quarry had blocked the door with the crate in an attempt to delay them, while making their escape through the workshop and up the ladder from there to the deck. They were taken completely by surprise when Neill and Sellars jumped on them from either side of the door. Each man wrapped an arm tightly round his adversary's throat and bore down, forcing him to his knees. The rifles fell to the floor and Caroline ran out and grabbed them.

"You can let go now," she told Neill and Sellars. They released their possessed colleagues, who got to their feet to find her covering them squarely with both weapons.

Grinning triumphantly, she brandished the two rifles like a western gunslinger. She tried to twirl one but it flew from her grasp and clattered on the floor, fortunately landing at Sellars' feet.

"Er, I think we'd better have those, Miss," he said. He picked up the rifle and then took the other from a reluctant Caroline.

In the generator room Chris and his companions heard the footsteps of the other two aliens draw closer and closer to their hiding place. The muzzle of an Armalite came into view.

Jamie Grant moved with surprising speed for such a big man. He thrust the cable against the barrel of the rifle. They heard a cry of shock and pain followed by the thud as the alien fell.

Robson, unarmed, paused uncertainly, staring down at the still form of his fellow alien. He heard movement behind him, and turned to see Neill, Sellars and Caroline coming towards him with their prisoners. At the same time Chris, Jamie and Co appeared from behind the generator and surrounded him. Jamie was brandishing the electrocuted alien's rifle.

"End of the line for you, I'm afraid," he said. "We're not letting the three of you out of our sight."

In the aliens' faces were rage and frustration, mingled with despair. Their breathing came in short, harsh gasps. Their bodies tensed visibly and for a moment it looked as if they were about to make a fight of it.

Then the possessed men threw back their heads and screamed. The noise was like that made by someone who'd just had a boil painfully lanced with a red hot needle. They jerked convulsively and collapsed in a heap at Chris and Jamie's feet.

Jamie knelt to inspect them. "Well they're alive," he said. The men's breathing was returning to normal and something in their faces was also changing, before Jamie's very eyes. Their expressions were more like those of normal men, albeit very unconscious.

Dr Kincaid was examining the electrocuted alien. "He's out cold, that's all. He'll live."

With all attention focused on the bodies on the floor, nobody registered the movement in the doorway. In a sudden rush which took them quite unawares, Charlotte and Sean dashed forward and snatched up two of the rifles from where the oilmen had put them down. The IPL employees whirled round. "Oh no," said Caroline. "Not you again."

Any move to grab the other rifles would have resulted in instant death. Dave took one and ripped out the firing mechanism from the other, rendering it useless.

"Who's going to be the hostage?" Sean asked Charlotte.

She nodded towards Caroline. "I've a score or two to settle with her."

Sean lunged at Caroline, grabbed her by the wrist and yanked her towards the door. Chris made to intervene but immediately Charlotte swung round to cover him. The three terrorists started to back out of the room with their captive, all the time keeping Chris and the oilmen covered.

"We haven't got an awful lot to lose," growled Jamie. "You're going to blow us all to bits anyway."

"Maybe so," Charlotte said. "But if you want to live a while longer, you'd be advised to wait for at least five minutes of it before coming after us."

The terrorists and their hostage disappeared through the door. Everyone listened to the sound of their footsteps gradually dying away. "We should have tried to jump them," said Jamie with a glance at Chris.

"There are precious few of us left as it is," Chris said grimly. "I've a better idea. I don't know how long we've got before that helicopter gets here but I suggest you lot concentrate on finding those explosives and getting rid of them. Meanwhile I'm going after our friends."

Charlotte, Sean, Dave and their captive burst out of the rig superstructure into the morning sunshine. At a gesture from Charlotte, they moved to stand behind the angle of one wall of a generator housing, out of sight from the helipad.

"Let's hope we don't have to bloody wait long," said Sean. A shadow fell over his face. "They may find the bombs and get rid of them."

"We'll have to take that chance," Charlotte told him. She glared at Caroline. "Don't you give us any trouble or you're dead."

"You need me to be converted," Caroline reminded her.

"I'll kill you if I have to." By way of emphasis Charlotte clicked the trigger of her Armalite.

She eyed Caroline thoughtfully. Not the sort to make a compliant hostage, in the long run. And they knew what happened if a person remained under the alien influence for too long. Then there was her general hatred of the woman.

Her eyes soaked up Caroline's beauty and she felt a pang of regret, not just at the thought of this one girl's death but at all she had turned her back upon.

Sean's voice cut through her thoughts. "So that thing you've got, what is it exactly?"

"It's the product of a civilisation far older and far superior to our own. Once we're safely out of danger, we'll set about making contact with them and then – "

She cocked her head, her eyes lighting up, and a broad grin spread across her face. Sean and Dave were grinning too. All three had heard the sound of a helicopter.

"Well, there's timing for you," Charlotte said, looking out over the sea to where a tiny black insect-like shape had just become visible.

Her fists clenched convulsively, and her slim body quivered with an almost childish excitement. Her mind was taken up with the thought of what would happen when she detonated the bombs. Simultaneously there would be a dozen explosions at points spaced roughly evenly about the rig. The effect of the combined blasts would be devastating. Those not killed immediately would die in the resulting fire or in the further explosion which would be caused when the blaze ignited the reserves of oil and gas on board Piper One. Walls would buckle, rooms be gutted, and pylons collapse into the sea. The main structure would remain standing, but reduced to a charred and blackened heap of metal.

She pictured the oilmen jumping into the sea, their clothes aflame. There they would drown, or be burnt alive as blazing oil poured onto the water and flowed over it to form a fiery skin.

Through the fabric of her wetsuit, her fingers touched the little black box in her pocket and stroked it lovingly.

"Keep out of sight until they leave the helicopter," she ordered Sean. She swung round on Caroline. "You tell them about those explosives and you know what'll happen."

They waited while the sound of the chopper's rotors grew louder and its pitch changed. From their hiding place they saw it hover above the landing pad, then descend. Its wheels touched the deck.

A moment later the door in the side of the helicopter, which was a Sea King, swung down to form a ladder, and a dozen armed policemen scrambled down it, Chief Superintendent Lewars in the lead.

At a command from Lewars they began moving towards the superstructure of the rig, tense and alert.

Then four figures entered their field of vision. Charlotte, Sean, and Dave with one arm around Caroline's body, gripping her tightly, and the other holding a rifle against her head.

"Stay where you are!" barked Charlotte.

The policemen stopped dead. Lewars swore softly beneath his breath.

Not far away, Chris Barrett peered out at the scene from behind a crate, taking everything in. "Throw down your guns," he heard Charlotte rasp.

Lewars was thinking on his feet. That the team should themselves be taken hostage would complicate whatever situation this was they had found themselves in. There was no telling what would happen; things would be completely beyond his control.

"What do you want?" he asked Charlotte.

"I said throw down your guns."

"You cannot expect me to do that. I can see that you have a hostage and am prepared to listen to your demands, but we are not surrendering our weapons."

For a moment they confronted each other in silence.

Chris knew there was no way the rig crew could get rid of all the explosives in time. Whatever he was going to do, he had to do fast.

Charlotte and Lewars were staring unwaveringly at one another, absorbed in their confrontation. He started to creep towards the helicopter.

Its two pilots remained in their seats, tensely awaiting developments. Chris moved round the other side of the craft so that it screened him from the terrorists' view. He banged on the cockpit window, and one of the pilots looked down and saw him. He mouthed at the man to let him in.

After a moment's hesitation, the cabin door was opened wide enough to allow him to enter. "What's going – "

Motioning to the pilots to keep quiet, Chris glanced towards the rear of the cabin. He saw the crate which had contained the policemen's rifles, empty now.

Outside, Charlotte had come to a decision. The guns didn't matter as long as they had their hostage. If the police opened fire on them, they would respond by shooting Caroline. They might be dead before they could do so. But there was a definite possibility she would be killed; and that was something all Lewars' training would have instructed him to avoid.

"I want you to give up your radios," she snapped.

No-one was to be allowed to inform the mainland of what was happening. She didn't want the authorities on their tail.

Lewars hesitated. Dave ground the barrel of his rifle against Caroline's forehead, his finger tightening on the trigger.

"All right," Lewars nodded. He'd guessed as soon as the situation became apparent that he'd have to make some concessions.

The squad took out their radios and flung them on the ground. While Dave kept the muzzle of his rifle pressed against Caroline's skull, Sean gathered them up and threw them over the railing into the sea.

"And any mobile phones you might have on you," Charlotte ordered.

Sean stiffened, and briefly the alien look appeared in his eyes again. "Our signal is still operating. It will neutralise all radio and telephone communications in the area."

"Well that's alright then."

"We're taking the helicopter," Charlotte announced. "Can you fly the thing, Dave?"

"Yeah, should be no problem. But it's a Sea King, needs two pilots."

Charlotte scrambled into the cabin. "Out," she snapped to one of the policemen. The man obeyed. "You, stay exactly where you are and do as you're told," she ordered the other.

Sean and Dave bundled Caroline into the helicopter, jumping in after her. Sean gave her a thump on the back of the head with the butt of his rifle and she slumped to the floor of the cabin, stunned.

The door was slammed shut, and the policemen on the deck looked at one another in silence as the rotor blades whirred into life and the craft lifted off.

Inside it, Charlotte contemplated Caroline's half-conscious body for a moment or two.

Then she made up her mind. "As soon as we're clear of the rig, chuck her out."

In his hiding place, Chris Barrett stiffened, his body transforming into a mass of tightly knotted nerve tissue.

The police pilot looked round sharply. Charlotte saw the movement, took in his expression. "Don't try it," she snarled.

"You need me," he reminded her. "Like you said, you can't fly this crate with just one – "

If he could use that bargaining counter to prevent them killing Caroline he could use it for any other purpose. "I'll take the risk," she vowed.

He knew she meant it.

Looking out of the window beside her, Charlotte watched the figures on the deck grow gradually smaller and smaller.

The helicopter banked, swung out over the sea. "Right," she said, and flung open the door. Sean began dragging Caroline towards it.

With a suddenness that made Charlotte jump, almost losing her balance, Chris leapt from his hiding place and cannoned into Sean, who let go of Caroline and reeled against the wall of the cabin. He followed up with a savage punch to the pit of the terrorist's stomach. Sean sank to his knees, his face going a sickly shade of green.

Caroline was shaking her head slowly as consciousness returned. She sat up and blinked, taking in the situation through bleary eyes.

"Don't move," an unpleasant voice snarled. Chris turned to find Charlotte had snatched up her rifle and was standing in front of him with the weapon aimed squarely at his heart.

"It's not a good idea to fire a gun on board an aircraft," he told her.

"Turn around," she hissed.

"You know that, or you'd have shot me already."

They stared at each other.

The police pilot was trying to decide if he should exploit the distraction, throw the helicopter about and make Charlotte fall over. Dave would counter his action, but one moment was all he needed.

Charlotte flicked off the safety catch of her Armalite.

She saw something in Chris' expression and started to turn. Then Caroline jumped on her back and wrapped one arm tight round her neck, jerking her head back. Charlotte dropped the gun and concentrated on trying to throw her off. Chris ran to help Caroline, only to be stopped as Sean, recovering his wind, jumped up and leaped at him. The two of them closed, lurching about the cabin in a grim dance, arms around each other.

Likewise Caroline and Charlotte were engaged in mortal combat. Charlotte seemed far stronger than a woman should be, and the look on her face, Caroline felt, would haunt her for the rest of her days, assuming they got out of this situation alive.

The police pilot realised he couldn’t do it now. A sudden lurch either way and it might be Chris or Caroline who fell, giving the advantage to their opponents. For the moment he concentrated on his job, which was to keep the Sea King in the air.

Caroline’s one thought was to stop Charlotte from detonating the explosives. She had no idea if they were clear of the rig yet, and couldn't exactly stop to look out the window. She guessed Charlotte must have some kind of remote control on her.

Charlotte grabbed a handful of her hair and tugged. She gasped in pain, but held on grimly.

She managed to thrust a hand into the pocket of Charlotte's wetsuit. Her fingers touched something hard and she snatched it out. It wasn't the detonator, it was the alien crystal. Since it wasn't what she was after, she dropped it and resumed trying to overbalance Charlotte.

"Look out!" shouted Dave as Chris and Sean, still locked in combat, staggered into him, jarring his arm. The control lever was yanked sharply to the right. The helicopter gave a lurch, swinging down and sideways; back towards the rig. Chris and Sean lost their footing and fell.

Charlotte seized one of Caroline's fingers and bent it back. With a howl Caroline let go and shot away from her.

Through the cockpit window Dave saw a crane loom up directly in front of them. Immediately he pulled the control column to the left, the police pilot following suit. The helicopter scraped against the jib of the crane and they heard the ghastly screech of metal twisting and crumpling.

On the deck Chief Superintendent Lewars' face tightened. A streamer of grey, almost colourless fluid was trailing out behind the helicopter. It had been perhaps a chance in a million but in the collision with the crane the flap over the fuel intake had been prised open and the end of a severed girder had got inside it and then, as the helicopter continued on its way, wrenched off the safety cap.

Charlotte glanced through the window, saw they were too close to the rig to detonate the explosives, and turned her attention to the fight. Chris and Sean, struggling savagely on the floor, rolled towards the wall of the cabin – and she saw the shattered fragments of the crystal, smashed to pieces when their bodies had landed on top of it.

For a moment she stared at its remains in cold, unbelieving horror, then let out a wavering, piteous wail.

With alarm Dave and the police pilot saw where the helicopter's second abrupt change of course was taking it. Towards the plume of flame that blazed from the side of the rig, burning off the excess gas.

In the same instant a wild, mad look flashed into Charlotte's eyes and she snatched up her rifle from the floor. Caroline saw her face and flung herself aside just as she pulled the trigger.

Charlotte blazed away at everyone and everything in sight, overcome with rage, hatred and despair.

Dave's hand had been about to close on the control lever and pull the helicopter away from its danger when several bullets slammed into the top of his head, ripping it to pieces. His body jerked, then slumped lifeless in his seat. The police pilot also fell forward, a little jet of blood spurting from his scalp. The continuing fusillade of bullets riddled the control panel, wrecking it.

Caroline threw herself down as the bullets ricocheted off the walls and ceiling. Chris felt Sean suddenly stiffen and relax his grip, sliding off him to crumple in a heap at the executive's feet. His shoulder was a mass of blood and shredded flesh.

Then the gun fell silent, the trigger clicking uselessly, the magazine exhausted by Charlotte's mad frenzy. Charlotte tossed the weapon aside.

And whipped the detonator from her pocket.

With a gasp of horror Caroline flung herself forward and grabbed it, struggling to pull the little black box from Charlotte's grasp. She could feel Charlotte's fingers on hers, trying to prise them off. She thrust her head up and butted the terrorist hard on the nose. Charlotte's grip slackened, but not enough for her to snatch the detonator away.

Then Chris joined her, adding his weight and strength, and managed to tug the detonator out of Charlotte's hand. He had to pull so hard that it shot out of his grasp and clattered on the floor.

Sean picked himself up, gritting his teeth fiercely against the searing pain in his shoulder. He stared wildly around him, and through the cabin window saw the flame of the burner right in front of them.

"Look out!" he shouted instinctively. "Look out!"

Desperate to gain Charlotte's attention, he ran into the fray of bodies, trying to pull them apart. For a brief moment Caroline and Chris were distracted.

Charlotte broke free of Chris' grip, and launched a savage kick at Caroline which caught her in the pit of the stomach. She lurched backwards, winded.

Chris smashed his fist into Sean's face in a powerful uppercut. The effect of the blow, on top of his injured shoulder, was too much for the terrorist and he folded in two and collapsed.

Charlotte glanced around for the detonator, saw no sign of the device, and began scrambling about in search of it.

Chris saw that Caroline, still winded, was in no position to help him. He snatched up Sean's rifle, aimed it at Charlotte and pulled the trigger. Nothing happened. Sometime back in the drill chamber, Sean had killed one oilman too many for Chris' purposes.

Lifting the rifle high above his head, Chris rushed at Charlotte and brought the butt crashing down on her skull. She slumped down and lay still.

He glanced at Caroline, who seemed to have recovered her breath. Shouting at her to find the detonator, he turned to deal with the terrorist pilot. He saw Dave's body lolling in his seat, and the flame of the burner about thirty feet away from them. The policeman was shaking his head and moaning; it looked like the bullet had merely grazed his scalp and stunned him.

But these things needed two pilots, didn't they?

Neither he nor Caroline had the slightest idea how to fly the helicopter. Even if they could steer it away from the flame there was still the problem of getting it down safely. And Charlotte had gone right over the edge.

He ran to the window and looked out. There was one chance; just one chance, and a very slim one. In a few moments the helicopter would pass over the roof of one of the buildings on the deck.

The jump would wind them, might break a bone or two, but he didn't reckon it'd be fatal.

They'd have to time it just right.

He ran and undid the policeman's seatbelt, lifting him to his feet. Still dazed, the man offered no resistance.

The helicopter brushed the rig's radio mast, tearing it from its mountings and bringing it down in a tangle of twisted metal and sparking cables.

"Have you found the detonator?" Chris shouted to Caroline.

"No!" she yelled back.

Incredibly, Charlotte was starting to stir. The blow had knocked her out only briefly.

For a giddy moment Chris' gaze darted between her and the view through the window. The flame seemed to fill the whole screen.

Would the oilmen have got rid of all the explosives? It was a possibility.

Not all, but maybe some. Enough to save the rig from total destruction?

The fourth Armalite, Dave's. He'd quite forgotten it. He could see it lying in a corner near the door.

But now even a second's delay could be fatal.

He acted on an impulse. Scrambling over to Caroline, he grabbed her by the shoulder and spun her round, pointing at the cabin window.

"We've got to get out of here!" He felt her freeze in horror as she saw their danger.

She hesitated briefly. Then they ran to the open door of the cabin and looked down. One corner of a surface of tarmac and concrete came into view below.

The policeman was standing beside them. He'd come round fully, seen the shattered controls and the looming flame and realised there was no point in hanging around.

"Now!" shouted Chris. Bracing themselves, they leaped forward into space, legs spread to cushion the impact.

Behind them, Charlotte had shaken herself fulyl conscious. She darted about in search of the detonator, the tears of rage and grief still shining on her face.

The force of their landing jarred Chris and Caroline's bones and drove the breath from their lungs. They tried to stand up, lost their balance, and rolled over. Chris raised himself onto one knee and twisted round, craning his neck to look at the helicopter. Only ten feet separated it from the flame and the distance between the two was rapidly closing.

They were almost touching.

Charlotte saw the remote control lying a few feet away, and dived for it.

Her fingers closed around the black box.

She stabbed at the button.

The policemen on the deck saw the helicopter explode, blasted into blazing fragments as a massive orange fireball engulfed it. Some of the pieces of burning wreckage landed in the sea, others rained down upon the deck. Chris and Caroline ducked as a particularly large one sailed over their heads.

The echoes from the explosion died away, and an eerie silence fell. Chris let himself slump back, letting out a long wavering sigh of relief. It was over.

He sensed the policemen running towards them.

He turned to his companion to find her nursing her ankle. She winced, face twisting in pain.

"Caz? You OK?"

"I think her ankle's broken," said the police pilot, who had survived the jump unscathed. Chris examined it gently, but knew there wasn't much they could do. "It'll probably have to wait, I'm afraid. There'll be plenty of wounded to see to. Doc Kincaid will have his hands full. Can you stand?"

She tried, but as soon as she put any weight on her foot a stab of searing pain lanced through her. He caught her as she collapsed and sat her down.

"OK, just stay right there."

"Are you OK up there?" Lewars shouted from below.

"Just get us down, would you?" Chris answered.

A couple of the policemen went off and found Jamie Grant and his men. The oilmen fetched a ladder and rested it against the wall of the outhouse. Chris slung Caroline over his shoulder and carried her down it.

He lowered her to the deck and turned to find Lewars standing next to him. "You're going to be stuck here for a bit longer, I'm afraid," said the policeman apologetically. "In the meantime, perhaps you could fill me in on what exactly's been happening."

Chris described the whole episode as best he could. Basically, he told Lewars, MacDuggan and his men had been hypnotised in some way, as had the terrorists, by an unknown agency which sought to sabotage the rig.

"Well I'm not sure I understand it all," Lewars said finally, "but it sounds as if you did very well, both of you."

Chris nodded his thanks. Caroline, nursing her wounded ankle, managed a weak smile.

They heard someone approach, and looked round to see Kenny and the others who had been taken over by the alien crystal, including the oilman they had electrocuted in the generator room, stumbling towards them. They were blinking and frowning in confusion, but the expressions on their faces were undoubtedly human.

"They're normal," Chris shouted in delight. "They're cured."

Kenny stared at the policemen, comprehension of his situation gradually dawning. His shoulders slumped and he sighed wearily. Lewars studied him with interest, taking in the combat gear he was wearing. He looked enquiringly at Chris, who nodded.

"I'm afraid I'm going to have to place you under arrest, Sir," he said solemnly. Kenny shrugged, and held out his hands for Lewars to slap the cuffs on. He wasn't quite sure what had happened to him after the incident on the deck, and wasn't too bothered. He'd expected it all to end in disaster anyway.

Dr Kincaid had already been tending Connell and the other wounded oilmen. Once he had seen to them he made his way above, where he put a splint on Caroline's ankle and otherwise attended to it. He told her he saw no reason why it shouldn't soon mend.

Chris clapped Jamie Grant on the shoulder. "It's over."

"How's the lassie?" Grant asked, concerned.

"I'll live," said Caroline faintly.

Chris told Grant all that had happened. "Now we've got to wait a few more hours before we finally get off this rig."

"No we haven't," Grant smiled, showing him Charlotte's radio which he'd recovered from Robson.

"You're forgetting, they were jamming the signal somehow," said Caroline. "Might as well give it a try, though."

Grant called the onshore base, and to their delight actually managed to get through. The interference had ceased.

Caroline called Chris over to her. "Are any of the injured people possessed?" she whispered. "And the ones who are back to normal – how do we know they'll stay that way?" She didn't fancy the whole business starting up again.

"I don't think they'll be causing any more trouble somehow," he replied. "And even if they do...I mean, people know now, don't they? *We* know."

He sat down beside her. Together they looked out across the grey sea, feeling their bodies relax after the strain of the last few hours. The sensation as the tension left them was exquisite, almost sexual.

There was a lot of tidying up to do on Piper One before they could leave, and they really ought to be lending a hand. But they simply didn't have any energy left.

Caroline was staring with dull eyes at the wreckage of the helicopter where it floated on the surface of the sea. Chris studied her face, trying to guess her thoughts. Its very impassivity was a sign of what she'd been through.

"Well, what are we going to say in our report?" he asked.

"If I start going on about aliens and stuff, Hennig will think I'm mad. He's already convinced I've got a screw loose. I don't think the workers will talk about it either." Caroline sighed. "Oh I don't know, I'm sure we can think of something between us."

She regarded the oil drum beside her. "You know, there are times when I hate this stuff."

"At least it wasn't boring," he said. "Apart from the drill bit."

"Eurgh," she replied, grimacing. She wasn't in the mood for jokes, and Chris' weren't generally regarded as the best in the office.

"Boring," said Chris. "Drill bit. Get it?" He laughed. "Drill-*bit*, you see? Boring…"

"Oh just piss off, Chris," she said.

"We managed to *rig* up a solution..."

She gave him a warning look, and he found he could resist the temptation to observe that everything had been oil right in the end.

"Sometimes you have to joke about things like this," he protested. "It's the only way to survive them. I know what you're thinking. "A lot of people have died and it's because of me." Well, it wasn't because of you. Only in one sense. You can't help the fact that...that *they* got the wrong end of the stick. Anyway, cheer up; you're going to be head of the company in a few years' time."

Do I want to be? she thought.

Chris' voice hardened as a sudden surge of anger overcame him. "Oh and by the way, I saved your life back there. Twice. You might be bloody well grateful."

She turned and looked at him sharply.

He knew why she didn't thank him. She was still affected by the horror of what she'd gone through, but couldn't bring herself to acknowledge it.

"In fact, I've saved it quite a few times in the past. But as I recall, you've only once said "thankyou." You make the odd little gesture occasionally, but that's all. I think once in a while I'd appreciate something a bit more explicit. And you know why you're like that? Because you can't admit that anything's happened to screw you up; that you're like the rest of us, scared shitless whenever it looks like you're going to die. You have to be bloody Superwoman. God, you really piss me off sometimes."

She looked shocked for a moment, then averted her face with a scowl.

For a few minutes they sat in silence, Chris staring blankly at the sea, Caroline sulking over what he'd just said to her.

Then, happening to turn her head, Caroline caught sight of the pile of dead bodies which had lain on the deck since the massacre that had taken place there. Bodies which only a few hours before had been living, breathing men and women, chatting and laughing together in the warmth of the bar.

A couple of oilmen appeared, each carrying several lengths of canvas sheeting under his arm. They knelt beside one of the bodies and she saw that each length was made up of several smaller pieces, sewn together to form a makeshift body bag. With respectful care, they started to wrap up their dead colleagues.

Her face crumpled and Chris saw the tears pour from her eyes. Immediately he wrapped his arms around her in a comforting embrace. He felt her body quiver with her distress. "Hey, it's all right," he whispered. "It's all right, it's all right, it’s all right..."

He held her until she seemed to have composed herself. "You OK?" he smiled.

"I will be," she sobbed. "I will be. I think."

She had not realised, with all that had happened within the last few hours, that they hadn't had any rest since being woken by the fire alarm. Now, triggered off by the sudden release of emotion, the delayed exhaustion caught up with her. Chris saw that her eyes were shut, and that she was very still, and for a moment he was worried.

Then, laying her gently to the deck and examining her more closely, he realised she had fallen into a deep, deep sleep.

*

The sun was sinking behind Piper One as the relief helicopter soared up from the deck into the evening sky. Chris cast a glance back at the rig. It looked an impressive sight, with the rays of the setting sun glinting off the massive structure, off its steel girders and stanchions and pylons.

Caroline was huddled at the back of the cabin, still feeling tired and sleepy. Through the window she watched the slate-grey sea roll by.

In minutes they had left Piper One far behind them. Soon they were passing over the rig where MacDuggan had stayed for a year. Glancing down at the vast rusting hulk, Caroline started a little. She thought she saw something, a figure of some kind, standing on the deck of the rig. The details couldn't be made out clearly, but it was large and close enough to suggest by its general look that it wasn't human. It seemed a bit too tall and thin, with more than the usual number of arms and legs.

She saw it for just the briefest moment. The next it had disappeared from view, as if it had jumped over the edge and into the sea.

For just a second she caught a glimpse of something vast and glowing beneath the surface; then it was receding rapidly into the distance, and in a moment she'd lost sight of the thing.

She felt Chris nudge her gently. "You OK?"

"Yes," she replied woozily. “Just thought I saw something." Before she could elaborate on the remark sleep had claimed her again, and she wasn't to awake until some time after they arrived back in Aberdeen.

*

"Well, I think that wraps it all up," said Marcus Hennig.

All damage caused during recent events on Piper One had now been repaired, and the rig was fully operational again.

The bodies of the missing workers had been recovered from the sea. Caroline thought of McGuinness, going timidly to her room to ask if he was off the hook. She was heartily grateful she'd spoken to him before he died and assuaged his worries.

Kenny had been sentenced to ten years in prison for his involvement in the incident. Information he gave the police had led to the exposure of the Children of Gaia, the breaking up of its infrastructure and the arrest of its leading members. There would, Caroline supposed, be other such groups.

Officially the events on Piper One, from the first act of sabotage to the attempt to blow up the rig, were due to terrorist activity, and it was as a result of that activity that MacDuggan and the other oilmen had died. There would clearly have to be considerable tightening of security.

"Well, I still don't quite understand it all," Hennig told Caroline, "but as long as there isn't likely to be a repeat of this incident I'm not particularly bothered.

"The people we've lost can easily be replaced. We know now there's nothing intrinsically wrong with having a small crew.

Automation works. So construction of the Piper Two rig can begin right away."

So I suppose everything's all right then, Caroline thought dully.

Two weeks later, in Hennig's office, the senior management of IPL held their regular monthly meeting to discuss future plans and current areas of concern.

Caroline waited until the end, when Hennig asked if there was anything else anybody wanted to bring up, then stuck her oar in.

"I think we ought to be doing more about renewable energy," she said. "After the South American business we've rather tended to put it on hold; now I think we could profitably look at it again. I feel it needs a bigger input from us. A bit more research, a bit more funding. I was wondering this time if we could set up a committee, maybe work jointly with other companies who've shown an interest in it."

Hennig frowned. "We already give a certain percentage of our profits to it."

Yes, and it's not enough. "I think we could increase that percentage. That's something the new committee could look at. It could oversee the implementation of a strategy by which we replaced a certain number of our enterprises by wind farms, say, to the maximum extent by which renewables can make a serious contribution to the energy needs we supply."

She awaited some feedback. The others mostly stared back at her blankly, none of them showing any great enthusiasm for the suggestion.

"Are you going to take it on yourself then, Caroline?" asked one executive.

"What, are you saying I'd have to?"

"Well, our hands are rather full at the moment," Hennig said. "There's the new projects in West Africa and Colombia, the European Reorganisation Scheme. I doubt if any personnel could be spared."

The unspoken message was clear; *it was your idea, you bloody well do it.*

"In any case, I wouldn't have thought it was your department," someone objected.

"It isn't anyone's, really. Nobody here's suggested this before, at least not recently."

Hennig frowned. "Well, if you're serious, I could always give some thought to it and see what comes up. But you'd better be careful; you're in danger of overstretching yourself, what with Personnel and PR already under your wing. If you were thinking of doing it full time, and on a permanent basis, you'd have to give up the IO post at least."

Caroline pursed her lips unhappily. She knew what it would mean if she gave up her troubleshooting activities. The IO job mattered a great deal to her. It meant a chance to see the world as well as to achieve things, and be appreciated for them, within a wider arena than just her own country.

But there was so much at stake. Vital issues which couldn't be ignored, and which required people to make a certain adjustment if they were to be resolved.

If it really is that important, she told herself, you should be prepared to go the extra mile for it; for the environment. Make the sacrifice.

But she couldn't do it. She just couldn't.

In the end, you're just like all the others, she thought. We're none of us prepared to give up our privileges, our creature comforts. Should we be condemned for that, or was it inevitable, an unalterable part of our nature? If so, what did that imply for our future?

"Are we all agreed on that point?" she asked them. "It's something I'd prefer to be sure of."

A dozen heads, Hennig's included, nodded more or less simultaneously. "I think you can be," he told her.

"Well, let me have a rethink," she sighed. “Obviously the question needs to be considered very carefully."

"Let us know what you decide," said Hennig.

With that, he felt able to declare the meeting closed, and everyone filed from the room, making for their respective offices.

"What's with the sudden interest in windmills and things, Caroline?" inquired a colleague as he fell into step beside her. "You gone green all of a sudden?"

Caroline didn't immediately answer him. They came to the door of her room. There, she hesitated a moment or two longer before speaking, as if unsure how to give expression to her thoughts.

"There was someone I felt I owed it to," she said, and then disappeared inside, closing the door firmly behind her.

www.ingramcontent.com/pod-product-compliance
Ingram Content Group UK Ltd.
Pitfield, Milton Keynes, MK11 3LW, UK
UKHW020130250726
13967UKWH00002B/569

9 780955 730344